WILL GALLOWS AND THE
SNAKE-BELLIED TROLL

WILL GALLOWS AND THE SNAKE-BELLIED TROLL

Derek Keilty

Illustrated by Jonny Duddle

First published 2011
by Andersen Press Limited
This Large Print edition published by
AudioGO Ltd
by arrangement with
Andersen Press Limited 2011

ISBN: 978 1445 820071

British Library Cataloguing in Publication Data available

Printed and bound in Great Britain by
MPG Books Group Limited

To my wife, Elaine, with love

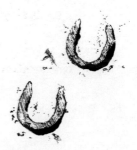

✶ THE GREAT WEST ROCK ✶

Mid-Rock City

Gung-Choux Village

Oretown

To Deadrock

The Wastelands

The West Woods

CHAPTER ONE

Gathering Storm

Tying up my horse, Moonshine, I walked slowly towards Oretown's sheriff's office. A display of wanted posters—a grisly gallery of wart-covered trolls and bulbous-eyed goblins—hung pinned to a notice board beside the office door. I plucked off the ugliest troll, rolling him up. Then, taking a deep breath, I pushed open the door.

Inside, the fat sheriff—a tin star pinned to his chest—was lounging with his feet up on the desk, and both he and a whip-tail goblin in the corner cell seemed to be having a competition to see who could snore the loudest. Nerves gripped me and I hesitated, feeling my heart hammer against my ribcage. I thought about leaving but realised that wouldn't get me answers, and I wanted answers more than I wanted anything else on the rock. I took a seat, staring at the soles of the sheriff's boots, and waited.

When the sheriff finally woke, he pushed up the brim of his hat and scowled at me. I unrolled the wanted poster of the ugly, snake-bellied troll on the table. It read:

The sheriff glanced at it. 'Just take it, kid, most folks don't even ask,' he growled. 'Then get lost.'

'It's not the poster I want, Sheriff Slugmarsh,' I replied. 'I . . . I need some information.'

'Information, what sort of information?'

'Whatever you can tell me about this murdering snake-belly.'

Slugmarsh belched loudly, tipping his hat back down over his eyes. A broad grin snaked its way across his face. 'Why? Are you going to bring him in for me?'

'Yes,' I replied, struggling to keep my voice steady.

The grin dropped off his face quicker than a rock bat off a mine-tunnel roof.

'I'm riding out after him,' I went on. 'I'm no killer, though. I'll be bringing him in alive.'

Slugmarsh pulled his legs off the desk and sat up to gawk at me. Then he laughed loudly, choking on his amusement, and spluttered and spat, trying to catch his breath.

I'd figured he'd do that. I sat silently,

waiting for him to finish.

'You're crazy, kid. Go back to school before I call the truancy goblin!'

'I'm almost fourteen,' I said, deepening my voice. 'I don't go to school.'

'Quit school to take up bounty slaying?'

'Pretty much, though I prefer "bounty seeker"—like I said, I'm no killer.'

Slugmarsh sat forward, reached into a drawer and pulled out bottle of Boggart's Breath whiskey. He took a long swig before slamming it onto the table, squashing a bug. To my bewilderment, the sheriff then drew his six-shot blaster and pointed it directly at me. 'If I thought for a second you were playing me for an idiot, boy . . .'

I felt my heart gallop even faster inside my chest and I raised my hands defensively. 'All I want is some information.'

Slugmarsh re-holstered the gun

and took another swig of liquor. He stood up and trudged over to check on the corner cell. The goblin still slept soundly on the lower bunk. I was sure I detected a jealous look on Slugmarsh's face. When he sat down again, he asked, 'You got a name?'

'Gallows, Will Gallows.'

'Gallows. I had a deputy name o' Gallows . . .'

'My pa.'

I stiffened as Slugmarsh leaned forward like he was inspecting me. His mouth dropped open and I saw a gold tooth glint among a mouthful of broken and missing teeth; his breath smelled of old socks. 'You're Gallows's boy?'

'Yessir.'

'Well now.' Slugmarsh took off his hat and swept a few sweaty strands of white hair up over his bald head, until they looked like a bunch of scorched tangleweed clinging to a rock. 'Last time your pa brought you in here, you were only half the size you are now.' He paused, dropping his eyes. 'Reckon it was around this time last year when he took a troll bullet and was killed in the gunfight at Pike's Ridge.'

'Murdered,' I corrected.

Slugmarsh nodded slowly. 'He was a good deputy, best I ever—'

'I know,' I broke in. I preferred not to talk about it. It was too painful.

Slugmarsh took a deep breath. 'Noose and his cronies came out of nowhere that morning.'

'I heard Pa shouted for cover. It wasn't there. He was let down.'

Taking a swig from his bottle, Slugmarsh offered it to me but I shook my head impatiently, waiting for his response.

'Boy, you got no idea what it was like. We were caught in a storm of bullets. Noose was like some trigger-happy demon. It was chaos. Couldn't hear yourself think above the noise of the shooting!'

I dropped my head. I was suddenly aware of the sound of grit chafing the window as a gust of wind kicked up dust from the street.

Slugmarsh stroked his beard. 'I'm starting to fear for you, boy.'

'Fear—why?'

'I'm beginning to think you might be serious about this. And cos I gotta hunch you're after more than just the bounty.'

'Noose Wormworx killed my father,' I choked, blinking away the swell of a tear. 'He should be brought to justice.'

Slugmarsh reached over to pat a huge awkward hand on my shoulder. 'Course he should, boy, but you think your pa would want you to follow him into the ground tryin'? Heck, you're only a kid.'

I felt my face redden. 'I'm not a kid. Besides, I've made up my mind.'

'Then you're crazy!' Slugmarsh

boomed, wheezing and coughing at his outburst. 'There isn't a posse on the rock stupid enough to ride out after that killer.'

Clenching my teeth, I rolled up the poster. 'I'd have preferred not to ask for help, but I figured as sheriff you might've at least pretended to be interested.' I made for the door. 'I'll see myself out.'

Slugmarsh put his head in his hands and breathed a long sigh. 'Spirit's sake, boy. What is it you wanna know?'

I stopped. 'Where is he?'

'Your guess is as good as mine.'

Reaching into a drawer, Slugmarsh pulled out a side-view map of the Great West Rock. He ran a dirty finger over the cactus-shaped world with its thick trunk and arms, on top of which were marked place names: Oretown, Mid-Rock City, Gung-Choux Village and others, all connected by a rail track that coiled around the outside of the whole of the West Rock. But it was on a dark cave in the middle of the trunk that his finger drummed.

'He's most likely holed up in the

The Great West Rock map showing: Mid-Rock City, Gung-Choux Village, Oretown, To Deadrock, The Wastelands, The West Woods

underground city of Deadrock. The place is full of outlaws. S'no place for an elf kid, though. If those snake-belly trolls get hold of you, they'll chew you up like bacca weed and leave you for dead. You ever seen a snake-bellied troll?'

'Not yet.'

'They are the evilest kind of troll you could meet and they ain't called snake-bellies for nothing; they got three, four, sometimes more real snakes pouring out of their guts, tongues flickering. Some folks say the snakes help the troll sense their surroundings, 's'why trolls can live in dark underground cities like Deadrock.'

I shuddered. I didn't need reminding how gruesome snake-bellies were; Pa had told me stories about them when I was a kid and given me nightmares. But I was determined not to let it put me off going after one.

'My pa told me the sheriff keeps records on all of West Rock's outlaws. I'd like to borrow whatever you have on Noose.'

'You think I'm running a library, kid. I can't let confidential records leave this office.'

Suddenly, there was a slight tremor. I noticed the whiskey swill in the sheriff's bottle. The second tremor made the floor jerk slightly. We stared at each other.

'Rock quake,' I breathed.

Rock quakes shook the town every so often but were becoming more frequent. Usually they were too small to do any serious structural damage, but there was always the worry that the big one was just around the corner. My grandma, Yenene, is always talking about how the tremors are signs that the rock spirits are angry at the way folks live their lives nowadays. And I usually try to change the subject before she starts going on about the good ol' days when she was a child growing up in Gung-Choux village. I'd overheard a couple of alchemists from Mid-Rock City discussing that they weren't tremors at all but the land sinking because of the mines inside the West Rock.

'Look, kid, I wish you luck, but I can't let you take those pap—'

Another big tremor hurled us both off our feet. Slugmarsh let out a yell as he rolled across the floor, crashing into the iron bars of the corner cell.

The goblin was flung out of his bunk, landing inches away from the sheriff. Chairs toppled, bottles smashed, a

11

filing cabinet crashed onto its side and its drawers opened, spilling out files. I flung my arms over my head to avoid injury.

'Moonshine,' I breathed. My horse was tied up outside, storms and quakes didn't usually spook her, though if a lump of roof landed on her . . .

Then, as suddenly as they had come, the tremors ceased.

I glanced over to the cell and gasped in shock. The goblin was wide-awake and in a calculated move, he let fly with his long wiry tail; it shot down the sprawled Sheriff's flank to his holster, coiling round the butt of the gun.

'Behind you!' I yelled, but the warning was hopelessly late. In a second, the goblin was armed and grinning.

Slugmarsh struggled to haul himself to his knees, but the six-shot blaster was already aimed at his head.

'Hands in the sky, Marshall!' the goblin shrieked, his rasping voice tinged with nervous excitement. Slugmarsh snarled at him but slowly raised his hands.

Next thing, the goblin swung the gun at me and for the second time that morning I stared into the barrel of the six-shot blaster. The goblin's eyes bulged beneath thin pointed ears. 'You, kid, get the keys from fatso's belt here and unlock the door real slow now, nothing fancy.'

Goblins are notoriously trigger-happy so I turned the key in the lock, real slow.

'Now, back off.' The goblin shoved open the cell door. 'I've had me a swell time, Sheriff,' he hissed, 'but I'm checkin' out. You'll understand if I don't leave a tip.'

'Your trial's in the morning. You could walk free. If you do something stupid they'll hang you.'

The goblin laughed like a Wasteland hyena. 'Since when did a goblin get a fair trial? You know as well as I do, they'll probably hang me anyways. No, I'll take my chances. Now, you two, in the cell. Move!'

It was then I noticed that the goblin's tail lay between the half-open cell door and the door jamb. I lashed out a

13

foot, kicking the cell door shut on the goblin's tail.

The pain must have been excruciating, judging by the wail he let out. Arms flailing to open the door and free his trapped limb, the goblin dropped the gun and I sprang on it like a pouncing wood panther. Now it was my turn. In seconds, I was back on my feet and, trembling, I pointed the gun at the goblin.

Slugmarsh smacked both thighs. 'Quick thinking, boy.' He held out his hand. 'Now, give me the gun.'

But I froze, my gaze darting between the two of them.

The goblin's eyes rolled in their sockets. 'Yeagggh! Stupid kid!' he cried, nursing his swelling tail. 'Give me that gun.'

I stepped back. 'Come any closer and I'll shoot!'

Face contorting, the goblin moved slowly towards me. 'You're bluffing, kid. You don't have the guts.'

I fired a round at the goblin's scrawny feet. 'Back off!'

The goblin shrieked, stumbling

backwards. 'Crazy kid! You could've blown my foot off.'

Slugmarsh cleared his throat loudly. 'I'll take it from here—before somebody gets shot.'

But I shook my head.

'I ain't asking. That's an order, boy.'

The goblin hissed at me. 'Hey, kid, I couldn't help overhearing your talk about Noose Wormworx. I could take you to Deadrock, maybe even help you find Noose—goblin's got no love for snake-bellies, you oughta know that.'

'I don't think so, I work on my own.'

I herded him back into his cage, then pointed the gun at the sheriff.

'Wha . . . you gone crazy?'

The poster of Noose had fallen off the table during the tremor and now sneered up at me. I swept my fringe up under my hat. 'No. It's just, like I said, I'd really appreciate borrowing those records.'

Slugmarsh's forehead and neck veins bulged to the point where I thought they might explode. He puffed and gasped like an old steam engine for a while then, still huffing, began poking

16

through the strewn leather-bound files on the floor with his foot. Growling, he kicked one of the thicker files over to me. 'Now, give me that gun.'

I lifted the file and blew off the dust. Then, grinning, I backed slowly towards the door, carefully stepping over fallen chairs and broken glass. At the last minute, I tossed the gun to Slugmarsh. 'Thanks.'

I ran out into the beginnings of a dust storm and untied Moonshine.

'What's going on? I heard a gunshot and screaming,' she cried, her nostrils flaring. 'I thought you'd been shot!'

'Shhh! Take it easy, Shy. Sheriff just wasn't too keen on me disturbing his nap.' I noticed her eyes were like saucers and I stroked her neck. 'You OK, that was a pretty big quake?'

'I'm fine.'

I checked the sky and frowned. 'Looks like a storm's brewing. Can't risk flying, you OK to ride back to the ranch?'

'Long as you tell me what's going on . . .' her voice trailed off as a couple of men rolled out of the nearby saloon and began staggering towards us. Men folk don't hold with talking to animals, saying that the Great Spirit created beasts to be submissive to folk and that they should be silent. But I am half elf, and elf folk have a strong bond with all animals. Critter chatter, as it's known on the rock, comes as naturally to me as eating and breathing.

My pa was human and my mother, who was a green-skinned elf, died when I was a baby. Since Pa's death, my grandma, Yenene, had looked after me. She was a she-elf with wizened, yellowish-green skin, rougher than ogre hide. She often told me that Pa knew well the perils of being a deputy but that upholding the law had been his passion and that there was no point getting all swollen with hatred about him being taken. My brown hair favours Pa, though it doesn't hide my long pointed elf ears. Pa punched a man once for calling me a half-breed.

'What kind of business you got with the sheriff? Are you in some sort of trouble?' Moonshine asked when the men from the saloon had gone.

18

I put Noose's file in the saddle pouch. 'I'll tell you on the ride back to the ranch,' I whispered, 'but only cos a sky cowboy should never keep a secret from his horse, and because I trust you not to breathe a whinny about this.'

Moonshine lowered herself onto her front legs and I swung into the saddle. Then we set off at a lope through the empty streets of Oretown, riding out towards the rock's edge.

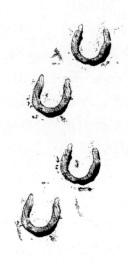

CHAPTER TWO

Troll Fishing

'You're what?'

'You heard.'

Moonshine flicked her ears. 'I heard, only I figured the dust this storm's kicking up is playing tricks with my ears. Going after your pa's killer—you serious?'

We were riding the path out of Oretown into open country. An angry dust storm blew grit in our faces.

'Shy, you've been my best friend for years now, you know I wouldn't kid about something to do with Pa,' I replied, pulling my bandana up over my nose.

'I know, 's'just I never heard you talk like this before. Sounds like a job for the sheriff, not you.'

'Slugmarsh's fat legs are glued to his desk. 'S'like he's too afraid of Noose to wanna do something.' A far-off tornado danced near the rock's edge.

The storms were always worse there, and Grandma said that when a storm threatened I wasn't to fly off the edge or even ride anywhere near it.

'Maybe he's afraid of him for good reason.'

'Guess I'll find out soon enough. Anyway, Pa used to say if you want a job done right, do it yourself!'

'Where will you go?'

'I'm still figuring out that part of the plan.' I dropped a hand to check the buckle on the saddle pouch. 'That's why I had to pay a visit to the sheriff's office.'

The dust storm passed over as quickly as it had come, and once again a ferocious sun beat down on the West Rock.

'C'mon, we can fly the rest of the way home.'

I spurred Moonshine on to a full gallop then gently tugged the reins. Even through the saddle I could feel her shoulder and flank muscles driving each downbeat of her powerful wings, like steam-engine pistons, lifting us off the ground to soar over the scorched landscape. Moonshine is a mute-winged windhorse, bred for strength and agility. Grandma says that a windhorse can turn in the air quicker than any other horse on the rock.

'You told Grandma yet?' Moonshine asked.

'Not yet.' It was a sticking point in the plan. Yenene was seventy-seven years old. The wrinkles on her forehead were proof that she'd had more than enough worries in her lifetime. Then there was her weak heart. Physicians from Mid-Rock City said it was a miracle it hadn't given out years ago. Yenene had told me that she wasn't going anywhere till I was all grown up and I'd taken over the running of the ranch. And even then she'd probably stick around some.

'I'm still figuring that one out too. I think telling Grandma's gonna be the toughest part.'

'Kweek-kik-ik-ik-ik!'

A couple of young thunder-dragons suddenly dived past us, chasing a flock of small birds. I watched them close in on their prey before unleashing jets of

22

fire, roasting the birds in midair.

'Kweeeeeeek!'

I whistled. 'Now, if I can catch Noose as easily as that.'

Down below, the ranch house and outbuildings of Phoenix Creek came into view, situated on a slight rise. Behind them a river of the same name twists like a clattersnake for as far as the eye can see. Landing, I swung out of the saddle and led Moonshine towards the paddock, where I removed the file from the saddle pouch.

'I'll see you after lunch, and remember not a word, y'hear?'

Shoving the file under my shirt, I entered by the back door and stole up to my room, taking care to keep out of sight of Grandma. I had some precious time off from chores until after lunch, which judging by the smell of chokecherry pie wafting up from the kitchen would soon be ready.

Expectantly, I thumbed the yellowing pages of the file looking for clues, something, anything that might help me track down Noose. Slugmarsh was right, Deadrock cropped up more than a few times. And I figured it sounded like just the sort of place Noose might be hiding. As I read, I made up my mind that that's where my search would begin. Turning a page near the middle, a loose newspaper cutting from the *Oretown Chronicle* slid out onto the bed. I lifted it, expecting it to be like the others that were pasted into the file—a story of another Noose murder or robbery. But curiously it contained nothing about Noose. Instead, I found myself staring at an old picture of Pa. I felt a rush of sadness mixed with an odd feeling that made the hairs on my neck prickle. In the picture, Pa stood next to a very smug-looking grey-haired elf who clutched a semicircular, brass-coloured object. The article below read:

QUAKE BREAKTHROUGH!

Story by Digger Scoops

Inventor, Eldon Overland, proudly displays his latest invention for measuring rock quakes.

Overland has devoted years to studying rock quakes and hopes that his investigations will one day help make things a bit less shaky for Oretown folk.

Pictured with him is his good friend Deputy Sheriff, Dan Gallows, who has promised Eldon the full support of the sheriff's department during his research.

Gallows and Overland

What was the cutting doing in Noose's file? Had it been misfiled? Had it come loose from another file? Something told me it was in there for a

25

reason. Eldon had gone missing around the time of Pa's death; they say he'd been doing experiments on the rock's edge when he was swept off a narrow ridge by a tornado. Without a second thought I carefully folded the cutting and put it in my pocket. It'd be good to have a picture of Pa with me and I could figure out why the cutting was in the file later, on my way to Deadrock.

Hearing Grandma holler that lunch was almost ready, I closed the file and hid it under the dressing table. As I did so I caught my reflection in the mirror and feigned a smile.

'Grandma, I gotta go to Deadrock for a few days to hunt down the biggest troll bandit on the rock.' My fake smile dropped and I sighed. Course there was no way I could tell her, but I did have an idea. Stretching, I took down a long canvas bag from the top of the wardrobe and busily loosened the strings. The fishing rod had been my father's and was made from bamboo with a silver reel.

'Troll fishin',' I breathed. I figured it wasn't the worst of ideas and was probably my best chance of a ticket out of Oretown, though I hated having to lie to Grandma.

Standing on a chair, I found the rest of the tackle, another canvas bag filled with spare reels and string, and a square flat tin that slipped from my grasp. The tin crashed onto the floor. Lead shot and fly bait scattered all over the place.

I was still picking them up when I heard Yenene's voice calling: 'Will, 's'that you?'

'Yeah.' I opened the door a bit.

'Spirits alive, I figured for sure we had a burglar, a sneaky whip-tail or a fat wood troll.' She lowered the sight of a shotgun from one eye. 'What are you doing? Your lunch's gonna be ruined.' She'd tied her hair back to prepare the food and a silky grey ponytail hung down to the bowknot of her apron.

'I was looking for something.'

'Looking for what?'

'My . . . fishing rod.'

Yenene put a hand to her hip, frowning.

'I've been thinking,' I went on, 'if

27

it's OK with you, 'bout visiting Uncle Crazy Wolf. He's been writing me to come for ages, says the fish are biting mad.'

'Fishing, eh? I got calves need branding and you want to gallop off to Gung River.' Her eyes narrowed. 'Can't understand the sudden interest.'

'It'd only be for a few days.'

'Ask me, that fool brother o' mine's got too much time on his hands.'

I didn't let up. 'There's a train in the morning. I could be back 'fore you even miss me.'

'Tomorrow! What about that broken fence over at Four Oaks?'

'I'll finish it today.'

'I don't know.' She leaned on the butt of the shotgun. 'Been too many quakes of late for my liking.'

'I can look after myself, Grandma.'

'Awww, I don't mean to sound like an old meany. Spirits know you work hard enough, just like your father. Maybe that's half my problem—I forget you're still a kid.'

I hate it when she calls me a kid, but I bit my lip. 'Please, Grandma?'

'Depends how you get on with that fence.'

'Does that mean I can go?'

'That means, it depends how you get on with that fence,' she said. 'Now come on down, your lunch'll be getting cold.'

* * *

I ate my lunch at the long wooden table in the kitchen: wild-rice soup followed  by a slice of chokecherry pie and honey. Grandma prepared dried-beef sandwiches and filled water bottles for the ranch hands. When I'd finished, I thanked her and got back to my chores.

Arriving at the paddock I called to Moonshine. 'We got us a fence to mend, Shy.'

Moonshine galloped over and almost pounced on me. 'Take me with you!'

'Well I'm not planning on *walking* to Four Oaks.'

'I mean on the hunt for Noose. I been thinking, if the sheriff won't help you then I will!'

'Heck, Shy, I don't even know if Grandma's gonna let *me* go yet, let alone take you with me. And you can be sure she won't let me ride off the rock.'

'So we take the train and I ride in the horsebox,' Moonshine's voice was pleading. 'I've heard stories 'bout bounty slayers and every single one of them had a horse. They say Scarface Charlie's horse could smell a bandit three miles away.'

'Dunno, it's complicated,' I said as we walked out of the paddock. 'Deadrock don't sound like the kind of place for winged-horses. It's inside the rock's belly, no sky for flying and dark, real dark.'

'Look, I know I'm not a cavalry horse like my pa, but it's in my blood. That's gotta count for something. You're bound to come up against a fight, a struggle. How do you expect to do everything on your own?'

'I'm not meaning anything against

you, Shy, but sometimes relying on folk's the worst thing you can do.' I thought of Pa and of the day we'd got word of his murder at Pike's Ridge, of his shouting for back up. 'In fights and struggles it's every man for himself in my book.'

Moonshine didn't relent even as I swung up into the saddle and we took

to the sky. 'That ain't the cavalry way o' things,' she argued. 'When my pa was in the sky cavalry he said that every horse and every sky cavalryman was part of a bigger picture, everybody pulling together just like them thunder-dragons we saw earlier.' Shy sure didn't let anyone forget the fact her pa had been in the sky cavalry—an army of brave soldiers under the command of the high sheriff, the ruler of the West Rock, who flew on highly-trained winged-horses. They are based in a fort in Mid-Rock City.

'I'll wait an' see what Grandma says.'

I worked hard mending the fence and it took me longer than I'd expected. I had a few other chores back at the ranch, but there would still be enough time to pack if the fishing tale had worked and Grandma had decided to let me go.

A mist had begun rolling in from the east—a yellow cloudy mixture of dust and moisture rolling across the rock. I was about to mount Moonshine and head back, when I noticed something in the rough country beyond the newly repaired fence.

'You see that, Shy?'

Moonshine lowered her neck to follow my gaze. 'Looks like a calf.'

I edged nearer. The brand on the calf's side, though faded, was clear enough. It was the brand of a Phoenix.

'S'one of ours.'

Unhooking a coil of rope from the saddle, I vaulted the fence, then crept closer, keeping low to the ground so as not to scare the calf.

When I was close enough, I let fly with the rope. It fell round the calf's neck.

'Hey, little buddy, lost your way? What are you doing wandering about out here all by yourself?' But, trembling, the young calf said nothing.

I smiled. 'Too nervous to critter chatter, eh?'

I noticed it was limping slightly and, gently pulling the rope, I threw my arms round the calf's neck to comfort it. Then, examining its hind leg, I said, 'You got yourself a little swelling there. We need to get you back to the ranch.'

I led the calf over to Moonshine who

jerked up her head, sniffing the air.

'What is it, Shy?'

'I think we might have company.'

No sooner had she spoke than I spotted something in the distance. Hazy shadows flickering in the molten heat, big shadows—pick-tooth wolves. 'Uh oh, we got company, all right,' I said, my heart thumping. We were isolated, miles from the ranch and unarmed. Holding the young calf near, I noticed its eyes were wide and frightened as though it too sensed the threat. With some effort I steered the calf behind a clump of brush, hoping the wolves hadn't spotted us. There was a danger the pack was heading to where the steers were grazing. I needed to hurry to alert Grandma and the other ranchers.

Suddenly the calf sprang from my grip. I tried to grab the rope but it skimmed through my hand, chaffing my palm. I winced with the pain. 'Darn! Get back here, you little demon.'

To my horror, the wolves froze—they'd spotted the calf.

I lay on my back, watching hopelessly

as the calf skipped further out into the open. I couldn't move. I needed to keep my distance in case I had to mount Moonshine for a quick getaway.

Moonshine paced nervously about. 'Don't like the look of this, Will, they're coming over.'

'Shhh, keep still.'

As the pack moved closer, I could see their mouths were stained red.

I sighed with relief. 'S'OK, they've just killed. Their bellies will be full— they won't eat for days now.'

Confidence bolstered, I made a bolt for the calf, grabbing it round the neck. Sliding one hand under its jaw, I twisted its head until it tumbled over. Then I tied its hooves together with the end of the rope.

A loud gunshot rang out and I whirled round to see my grandmother fly out of the mist, her gun held high.

The wolves ran off at breathtaking pace, howling loudly.

A flurry of wing beats stirred up the dust as she landed. 'You all right, son?'

'I'm fine, Grandma, but you needn't have wasted a bullet. They just killed.

They're probably looking for shade to sleep it off.'

'You been out here a long time, I figured I'd come check on you.' I watched her peer at the mended fence. 'Looks like you done a fine job.'

'Thanks.' I gestured to the stunned-looking calf. 'This little fella's got himself a limp, I'm taking him back to the ranch.'

I gently lifted the calf and laid her in front of the saddle. Moonshine shot her a testy glance. 'Watch the coat with those hooves, y'hear?'

Then we all took to the sky.

"Bout this fishing trip,' Yenene began, wrinkled fingers expertly handling the reins to keep her mount below the mist and alongside Moonshine. 'I've baked some pies— your Uncle Crazy Wolf's favourite— not that he deserves them, ol' fool would never think of boarding a train to come pay me a visit. Anyways I'd like you to take them with you.'

'Y'mean I can go?' I cried.

The corner of her mouth curled up in a rare grin. 'On one condition, you bring me back a nice fat gutfish.'

'Oh I will, Grandma,' I said, Noose's face flashing through my mind. 'I plan on catching me the biggest, ugliest fish you ever set eyes on.'

'Just promise me you'll not overstay your welcome.'

'I promise.'

I noticed Moonshine nodding her head frantically and decided some company might be a good idea. 'I know I'll be taking the train, but be OK if Shy here comes along with me?'

'Long as you remember 'bout not riding off the edge when there's a storm threatening.'

'Thanks,' I replied, and Moonshine whinnied with delight.

We soared over Tombstone Wood, the shorn remnant of a once vast forest. I could just make out the rotting totem pole in a small clearing. Yenene had told me stories about how, hundreds of years ago, it had been populated by elf folk who had at one time lived on the western arm. That was until men, fleeing the bitter troll wars of the West Woods, had climbed the rock and run the elf folk off the western arm. Behind the wood were rolling hills pocked with caves. They reminded me of the enormous cave containing the evil underground city of Deadrock that I soon planned to visit.

'Grandma, you ever been to Deadrock?' I asked, trying to sound casual.

Yenene shook her head. 'Closest I ever been to that spirit-forsaken place was when I rode with your pa down to Pike's Ridge the time that fool elf Eldon was wasting all his spirit-given time measuring the rock quakes. Just being near Deadrock sent a chill down my spine. I remember seeing the Flyer go by without a soul on it and thinking, *Well that makes sense.*' Who'd wanna catch a train to a gangster troll-hole like that place?'

'Wasn't Eldon afraid of being down there?'

'Your Pa warned him he'd need to be careful, but Eldon didn't seem to care. He was too wrapped up in all his crazy gadgets and experiments. If only your Pa hadn't ignored his own warning and gone back that day.'

'Why'd Pa have to go back?'

'Eldon wanted him to bring Sheriff Slugmarsh down, something about a new discovery Eldon had made. Never did find out what all the fuss was about. Your pa had only just arrived when Noose flew outta the steam of a passing train, out on a hold-up. He saw the lawmen and . . . well ain't good going over it all again.'

I swallowed a lump in my throat as an image of Pa drifted through my mind. I checked my pocket for the cutting from Noose's file, feeling the folded paper.

'Do you really think a tornado swept Eldon off the ridge?' I asked.

'Your guess is as good as mine. Sheriff said he wasn't there when your Pa and him arrived that day, and no one has seen him since.'

Landing near the paddock, I patted Moonshine then took her by the reins. One of the ranchers grabbed the calf to tend to it. 'I still say Slugmarsh ain't worth much in a gunfight, what with being Sheriff and all.'

'Slugmarsh said Noose had a mob with him, says they had no chance.' Grandma pulled my hat over my eyes. 'Come on now, reckon you deserve a big slice of fresh baked pie, one pie will be plenty for your uncle.'

*   *   *

The moon was high in the sky, bathing the West Rock in a pale, ghostly light when I approached the stable barn. I'd one last thing to pack, only I didn't want Grandma or anyone else to know about it.

The air inside the stable was laden with the sweet smell of hay and leather mingled with the sweat of the horses. I greeted them all as I passed their stalls.

Moonshine snorted, flicking her ears at the sound of my voice. 'Will, we going for a ride? There's a bright moon tonight.'

''Fraid not, Shy, I have to get something.'

'For the hunt?' said Moonshine excitedly.

'Yeah. You all set?'

41

'You bet. Been the only thing on my mind all day. When do we leave?'

'Tomorrow.'

'Great. No hanging around.'

'Best if we go while Grandma's in a mind to let us.'

'Well, don't worry about me, I won't hold you back. I'm ready to go tonight if you want.'

I backed up, finger to my lips. 'Hush now. Don't give me away. Grandma don't know I'm here.'

When I was little I'd been afraid to go inside the barn. The walls were decorated with dozens of old elf artefacts Grandpa had collected. There was a wooden drum with a painting of an elf warrior on a rearing horse surrounded by flying arrows. Behind that sat an old painted rock-buffalo skull that still made the hairs on my neck stand up.

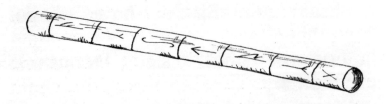

Climbing on a stool, I took down a beautiful carved wooden blowgun about the length of my arm. I put it to my lips and blew softly. My breath rushed silently through the small channel. Beside it was a beaded leather pouch, which I also took. Opening the pouch I counted six pointed darts, splinters of river cane topped with the down of an eagle. I rummaged in the bottom of the pouch and took out a small glass jar full of green gel. Bait!

The writing on the jar was Elfin but I knew exactly what it contained— poison from the sweat of the wood frog. A dart tipped with even a tiny bit of the poison would send its victim into a deep, delirious sleep that would last a full day. I'd been practising for weeks now but there was time for one last go. I placed one of the darts in the channel and aimed the blowgun at the target: a little circle I'd drawn in white chalk on a distant wooden pillar. The dart whistled through the air and speared into the centre of the target.

Moonshine stood watching, her eyes growing wider till, excitedly, she blurted out, 'Now I get it. You're gonna kill him with a poison dart?'

'Shhh! I'm not killing anybody,' I chided. 'I'm putting him to sleep so I can get him aboard the Flyer and up to Mid-Rock City jailhouse.'

'How we gonna move a big, fat, drugged-up troll?'

I grinned. 'Guess that's where you come in. I'll be throwing him over your saddle just like that calf earlier.' A look of horror spread over Moonshine's face till I added, 'Don't panic. I saw a picture in the file of Noose holding Gus Markham from the mercantile store in a throat lock. They're standing together only Gus, see, is taller than Noose and I'm 'bout the same height as Gus, so I reckon Noose can't be any bigger than me. Maybe he has some dwarf blood in him.'

I pulled the dart from the pillar and put it back in the pouch with the others. Then I hid the blowgun as best

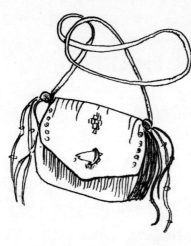

I could under my coat.

'See an' get plenty of rest, Shy. We got a big day tomorrow.'

I stole back to my room, careful to keep the blowgun out of sight. I packed it in the canvas bag alongside the fishing rod. Would a few days be enough? I had to make sure it was. I'd have to work fast to track down Noose and bring him in.

My packing finished, I yawned then climbed into bed. I had an early train to catch.

CHAPTER THREE

The Iron Horse

Oretown station had the unenviable honour of being the smallest and grubbiest station on the rock. The rock quakes were really taking their toll. A ramshackle wooden hut, with broken windows and a clock that never kept time, offered some shelter. Course, the

roof had so many holes that if it rained you still got soaked. The platform was dusty and strewn with empty bottles and newspapers that whirled in circles from pockets of wind that formed here and there.

A family of folk stood with suitcases and wooden crates. One of the kids, when he came over to pet Moonshine, told me that the rock tremors were getting too much for them so they were moving to Mid-Rock City. It was becoming a familiar story.

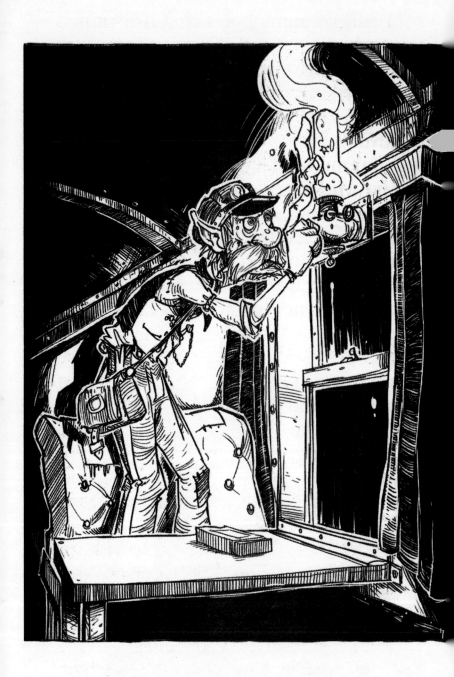

'Train's coming!' I cried, hearing a faint whistle. 'You sure you're still OK 'bout coming, Shy?'

Moonshine tossed her head, pricking her ears. 'Are you kidding? I still can't believe you were thinking of going without me.'

The Mid-Rock City Flyer came into view, snaking round the bend inland from the rock's edge, pulling a string of carriages.

I felt my heart thud like a green-skinned-elf peace drum. The Flyer always gave me a buzz of excitement. When I was younger I used to sit for hours with Pa, just watching trains thunder in and out of the station.

The steam locomotive, like some huge huffing, puffing beast, roared towards the tiny station. I wondered how Yenene could hate trains. 'Darn nuisance iron horses,' she called them, and had vowed never to ride in one. Steam and smoke spewed out of the stack in great clouds that could sometimes twist into shapes. Years ago I'd had nightmares for weeks after I saw the ghastly shape of a demon's face

49

scowling at me from the smoke. Pa told me I was imagining things.

The train groaned to a stop, iron wheels protesting against the poorly-maintained track. Rock tremors and a boom in rail travel were taking their toll on the ancient metal. I led Moonshine towards the horsebox, triggering the conductor to alight from a neighbouring carriage and begin sliding back the horsebox door. I felt a dribble of sweat meander down my face. Nothing to do with the ruthless heat, but this was it. Once I boarded the Flyer, the hunt was on!

Seeing the horsebox empty, I addressed the conductor. 'Sir, she's gonna be all alone in there. Could I stay with her?'

''Gainst the rules, son,' the conductor replied, lowering the ramp. 'Folk have to ride in the carriages.'

I led her into the horsebox. 'Sorry, Shy, but it won't take that long getting to Deadrock.'

I walked down the platform and, boarding an empty passenger carriage, I took a seat at a window. The next thing, a whistle blew and, with a jolt, the train began to move off.

I held the rod and bag tightly beside me. It didn't matter that I couldn't reach the luggage shelf without standing on the seat, as I had no intentions of letting them out of my sight. They were all I had now.

Oretown landmarks flashed by the window: the bank, the mercantile store, the sheriff's office. I guessed Slugmarsh would probably be asleep, his legs glued to the desk, as usual.

After a short while, an old elf wearing a neat green and silver Railroad Company waistcoat entered the carriage, carrying a box of matches over to the lamp above the window.

'Going to get dark soon,' he muttered. 'We're headed for a tunnel.' The elf looked even older than Grandma but was obviously too poor to give up working. I admire elves above all the rock folk, even more than humans. They are a proud, hard-working race. Not to mention the fact I am half elf myself.

Curiously, the elf didn't open the

51

box of matches but, standing on the seat, cupped one hand over the glass cover. Immediately smoke began to trickle upwards from the wick, seeping through his fingers. Moments later, a tiny flame danced in the smoke. *Elf magic*.

'I wish I could do magic like that,' I told him. 'But my grandma says I can't on account of me only being half elf.'

'With respect, your grandma is wrong. She's probably just afraid.'

'Afraid of what?'

'All magic has its dark side,' he said solemnly, 'but in the right hands it can be a power for much good.'

'My Uncle Crazy Wolf is the medicine mage of the Gung-Choux tribe. Once when we were out fishing, he shot a fireball the size of a watermelon from the palms of his hands. Course, I never told Grandma.'

The elf's bushy eyebrows leaped up his forehead. 'That's quite something. As a young elf, I was apprenticed to a medicine mage for almost a year before I ran away to work for the railway. That's where I learned how to conjure the flame.' He glanced forlornly at the lamp then turned to leave. 'Sometimes I wish I'd stuck at it. It's a noble vocation. History books say it was a medicine mage who kept the human invaders at bay for so long on the western arm, hundreds of years ago.'

'Thank you,' I called after him as he shuffled out of sight. I wanted him to stay and tell me more about elf magic, and I reckon he would've if he hadn't been so busy.

A short while later the train plummeted into the Mid-Rock tunnel. The noise level doubled, echoing off the rock. I stared into the blackness. And stared. And then two eyes, in a skull, glowing white and huge, stared back at me from the gloom, accompanied by a noise like shrill laughter. My blood ran frost-cold and I pushed back into the seat. A ghostly clawed hand came straight through the window as if the glass wasn't there, and groped about the carriage. The flame flickered in the lamp, almost going out, and the hand seemed to shrink back. More laughter and I didn't dare breathe. Then it was gone. The lamp caught and burned brighter again.

I was relieved when the train came out the other end, the daylight dazzling my eyes. The lamplighter shuffled in again, this time carrying a tin snuff. Once more, the implement he carried remained by his side as, with the wave of his empty hand, the flame extinguished.

The elf rolled a milky eye at me. 'You OK?'

'There was something in the carriage, a hand . . .'

He nodded. 'There are evil spirits called mine wraiths lurking in the bowels of the rock. You *should* make time one day to learn elf magic, it will help you. Especially since your uncle is a mage, the blood line is most likely strong. You could be of great benefit to your people.'

I was considering this when the elf made the snuff vanish. Then with a wink he added, 'By the way, you didn't see any of that—the Railroad Company boss, like most human folk, hates magic.'

When the elf left, I stared out at the dry scorched landscape of the eastern arm top. Up ahead I saw the conical wigwams and towering totems of Gung-Choux Village. A short while later the Flyer was steaming a path right between them. A green-skinned elf riding a beautiful chestnut windhorse, chased playfully alongside the train, and I thought about Moonshine; I hoped she wasn't too uncomfortable or frightened riding in the horsebox.

I slid down on the seat as the train approached Gung-Choux station. However unlikely, I couldn't take any chances on Uncle Crazy Wolf being about. The conductor shot me a strange glance as he passed but I stayed put.

The train pulled out of the station and, head resting on the window, I stared for a long time at the bare rocky landscape and thought about nothing. I was tired. I'd hardly slept last night. And so I did something I'd vowed I wouldn't do. I fell asleep.

Sometime later I woke up to find

someone had placed a cushion at my head. I clutched frantically for the bag and rod. They were gone. Holding my breath, my eyes shot round the empty carriage, up to the luggage shelf. They were there. I breathed again. Someone was being a bit too attentive. The lamplighter maybe, or some other passenger who had since got off. My relief though was quickly shattered by another thought. Where was I? What if the train had already passed through Deadrock and I'd missed my stop? I stared out the window. The train was travelling along the rock face, a sheer drop stretched for miles below into the wastelands. I opened the carriage door and hurried down the narrow corridor to ask someone. The train was now almost empty except for a few forest-dwelling folk, most likely on their way to the West Woods. I spoke to one forest dweller whose blank expression told me he didn't speak my language. Then I heard voices nearby and headed for the next compartment.

A gang of whip-tail goblins sprawled over the seats drinking Boggart's

Breath and playing snake poker. I froze, instantly recognising one of them as the goblin from Oretown jailhouse. He caught my eye and sneered, 'Well now, what have we here?'

The whip-tail slowly rose to his feet, a grin spreading over his face. 'So you're going to Deadrock. You got more guts than I figured you for. Come in and join us, Deputy.' The grin turned quickly into a snarl as the goblin coiled his tail round to show me the swollen lump. 'Surprised to see me, hero boy? Wondering how I managed

to check out?'

I couldn't speak.

'Then I'll tell you,' he went on. 'Seems I was wrong about them hanging me. Especially since the sheriff's key witness met with a little accident.'

The goblin lashed out his tail and struck me in the face. It stung painfully and I collapsed onto the floor.

The goblin's cronies laughed raucously. 'That'll teach the elf scum,' drooled one of them.

'Y'know, boys, I don't think it will. This kid's so stupid he needs to be taught more than just one lesson.' The goblin moved towards me, laughing till saliva dribbled down his chin. I rolled over and, scrambling to my feet, stumbled back along the carriage, crashing through the sprung doors separating the compartments and running.

'Nowhere to go, kid.' The goblin sneered, sounding like he was in no hurry to stride after me.

I came to the last compartment. A sign on the metal door read:

DANGER
DO NOT OPEN

I didn't hesitate. I slammed both hands on the door bar and burst outside. Wavering, I stopped dead, staring down at the coupling between the two carriages.

Below, the track blurred past making my head spin. The Flyer was steaming at top speed. I figured it was about a good jump's distance to the other carriage, but if I misjudged it or missed getting a grip on the far door . . .

Glancing back, I saw the goblin about a compartment's length back, strolling slowly and laughing. Then, without looking down, I jumped. I cleared the coupling but missed the door bar. I grabbed blindly at the air and just caught the rail of a steel ladder that ran to the roof.

'Hey down there! You gone crazy?' a

voice yelled above me.

I looked up and saw a dwarf girl about my own age leaning over the carriage roof.

'I'm being chased!' I blurted out.

'Chased! Well, why didn't you say so? Quick, climb the ladder.' The dwarf extended a hand. 'C'mon!'

I figured I'd nothing to lose. I climbed the ladder to the beckoning stranger and, clutching her stubby fingers, hauled myself onto the roof of the train.

'Now pull the ladder, it'll come off,' the dwarf instructed, grabbing one end.

We both tugged the ladder. 'It's stuck,' I gasped.

'Stupid thing's rusted tight in the

60

rain. Yank it, hard as you can. C'mon, we can do it.'

I tugged again with all the strength I could muster. One end jarred loose, then the other, and we drew it up and onto the roof. I fell back gasping.

The girl leaned forward to peer down at me and I found myself staring at two of the palest green eyes I'd ever seen. They were set into a dirty, round face topped with a tousled mop of black hair.

'W . . . Who are you?' I asked.

'Name's Jez,' said the dwarf, grabbing my hand to shake it vigorously, 'and I'm mighty pleased to meet you.'

'My name's Will,' I replied. 'What are you doing on the roof of the train?'

'Getting me some fresh West Rock air, that's what.' She grinned. 'I work in Deadrock Tin Mine and every so often I steal up on the roof of the Flyer—reminds me there's still a world out there with real air and eagles and moon coyotes. Can't understand why everybody don't climb up here instead of sitting in them stuffy compartments.'

She glanced over the carriage. 'Hush! Carriage door's opening.'

CHAPTER FOUR

A Dwarf Named Jez

Down below I heard the carriage door open, then drunken laughter, a noise like spitting and the goblin's voice hissing, 'Looks like you learned your lesson after all, dung fly.' More manic laughter and then the door slammed shut.

Jez drew back from the edge of the carriage and turned to me. 'He's gone. Mad-looking varmit, too—you must've rattled his cage pretty bad.'

'Thanks,' I said as a strong gust of wind persuaded me to clutch onto a rail that ran along the edge of the carriage top. 'But it was a rock quake rattled his cage. I just caught his tail in one.' I stared at Jez for a while before asking, 'You're a dwarf, right?'

'Prairie dwarf, if you please,' she replied, squinting back at me. 'You look like a human kid 'cept I ain't ever seen ears that size on a human.'

63

'My pa was human; my ma was a green-skinned elf.'

'Was.' Jez dropped her eyes. 'That mean they're both dead?'

I nodded.

'Mine too. My pa was shot dead trying to break up a saloon brawl and my ma died soon after, folks say of a broken heart.'

'Did you say you work in Deadrock Tin Mine?'

'Yup.'

'S'where I'm headed.'

'If you're smart you'll stay on the train.'

'Why?'

'Deadrock's an evil place—full o' slimy snake-bellied trolls.'

We sat silently for a moment staring out at the sky, then I decided it was time to make a move. 'Thanks for helping me but I gotta go. My bag's back in the carriage.'

I felt Jez's eyes follow me as I pushed the ladder back over the side and began securing it to the carriage top. 'I'm sure that goblin's still prowling around down there. What if he finds you? You might not be so lucky next time!'

'I haven't got much choice—I need my stuff.'

'Ain't meddling, but be safer if you just lowered yourself through the carriage window. I got me a length of rope, then you could get your stuff and bring it up top again.'

I thought about this. It did make sense to stay out of the goblin's way for the rest of the journey, though I wasn't sure if Jez's plan sounded any less dangerous than tackling the goblin.

'How do I get in the window?'

'They're top opening, you can shove 'em down with your foot.'

'All right then, I'll do it,' I said. 'Where's the rope?'

Jez untied an old length of rope from around the rail. 'I use it to hang onto; it can get pretty breezy up here.' She glanced over the side of the train before adding: 'Speaking of which, you better hurry. There's a tornado skirting around the bottom of the rock, be whipping its way up here soon enough.'

I made the jump across the carriage

coupling without a hitch, then tied the rope to the rail above where I figured my seat had to be and pulled, testing the knot for strength. Taking a deep breath, I slid over the side of the carriage. A strong east wind caught me as I dropped over the side and I swung like a hanged man on a gallows. Fumbling about, I got a foot on the top of the window, then pushed it down fully. Carefully I climbed down the rope until I was level with the window, then I pulled myself inside. My luggage was still on the shelf and standing on the seat I grabbed it, slinging the bag and blowgun over my shoulder.

I was about to climb back out the window again when someone banged into the compartment door. Spinning round, my blood ran ice-cold—it was the whip-tail outlaw. The goblin looked drunk and, holding up a bottle of Boggart's Breath whiskey like a trophy, sang a tuneless guttural goblin song. He peered into the carriage; face contorting as he struggled to focus. I turned quickly to look out the window.

Seconds later the goblin shoved open the door and stood there swaying. 'Wha . . . I thought you were dead . . . fell off the train . . . liddle trickster,' he slurred.

I slid my hand into the bag and clutched a poison dart. 'Back off and you won't get hurt.'

The goblin burst into ear-splitting laughter, his tail flailing on the floor. 'You think you can hurt me, do you?'

Fumbling in the bag, I opened the lid of the poison and, feeling my way, stuck the tip of the dart into the gooey mixture. I'd just replaced the cap when the goblin lunged at me. 'You're coming with me.'

The goblin grabbed me by the hair, but as he did so, I unleashed the dart, plunging it into his fleshy under-arm. He let out a shrill scream, recoiling in pain. He dropped the bottle of Boggart's Breath, which smashed, filling the compartment with the strong stench of whiskey.

'You little rock slug, I'm gonna make

you pay for spilling my . . .' his voice trailed off as the quickest most potent poison on the rock surged through his veins, galloping into his brain, shutting it down. The goblin's eyes danced in his sockets and he slumped onto his knees.

Jez chose that precise moment to lower herself down the rope and stare into the compartment. 'More goblins,' she gasped. 'They're multiplying. Are you OK?'

I stepped out of the way as the goblin splayed at my feet. 'I'm fine; I think he got the point.'

'That the varmit who was chasing you?'

'Yeah.'

'Are you in some kind o' trouble, Will?'

'No, he's just sore cos I helped keep him behind bars a while longer,' I explained.

'Well, I'll be. . .' said Jez, a twinkle in her eye. 'You're a regular l'il deputy, ain't ya?'

I grinned, hoisting myself through the window. The goblin, instead of falling flat on his face, must've found a sudden stash of failing strength. He sprang for my feet as they ascended out the window but his judgment was way off. Arms outstretched and tail lashing, he leaned after me. 'Ssssslug!' he cried. But he leaned too far and, losing his balance, tumbled out. I gasped as the goblin plunged down the rock towards the Wastelands.

Back on top of the train the wind had picked up, whipping round us. I shivered, unable to get the mad goblin out of my mind.

Jez suddenly sat up, eyes scouting the rock's edge ahead. 'Boggarts' britches I'm nearly forgetting 'bout my stop!'

'Are we coming into Deadrock?' I asked hopefully. I thought about Moonshine cooped up in the horsebox and hoped she wasn't getting bumped around too much.

'I ain't going to Deadrock. I'm getting off near Pike's Ridge.'

Pike's Ridge. The name jolted me from my thoughts.

'Train don't stop, of course, that's why I gotta pay attention,' Jez went on.

'Say, what's the matter with you? You look like you just tasted sour milk.'

'My pa, he was murdered at Pike's Ridge.'

'I'm sorry.'

'Wasn't your fault.'

'I know, I guess I just heard folk say sorry when . . . well you know.'

I nodded. I'd been thinking a lot about Pike's Ridge over the past few days but hadn't really planned on visiting the place. Till now that was. It did seem like a good starting point to the hunt, to see the place where Pa had been shot. There might be some clues as to exactly what happened there. Maybe even clues to Noose's whereabouts.

'The train doesn't stop?' I said, suddenly taking in Jez's earlier comment. 'So what are you gonna do— jump?'

The rock face raced by, at times it was almost close enough to touch. Jez nodded. 'Ain't as hard as it sounds. Train slows up a fair bit on the bend and at one point it passes within a cowboy's chin whisker of the ridge—all it takes is a well-timed jump into a big bush of tangleweed.'

I looked across the rock to see the tornado spiralling downwards, moving away from the rail track. My thoughts spiralled with it for a while then I announced, 'I'm not following you or nothing but I've a mind to get off too at Pike's Ridge.'

'Thought you were going to Deadrock.'

'I am, later. Be OK if I came with you?'

'Side of the rock belongs to everybody,' she shrugged. 'Though if you're thinking Pike's Ridge is some kinda town, you're wrong. It ain't nothing but scorched rock, tangleweed and some funny-looking twisty trees.' Raising a squat finger, she pointed up ahead. 'There, see that big ledge sticking out? That's it. You oughta toss your bag first . . .'

'Not sure about jumping,' I broke in. 'Sounds a bit dangerous, if it's all the same with you.'

'You ain't got much choice, 'less you gotta better idea?'

Lifting the rope, I began crawling in the direction of the horsebox. 'I think I might have.' I grinned. 'Instead of jumping, Jez, how'd you like to fly?'

CHAPTER FIVE

Pike's Ridge

Yet again, I found myself sliding over the side of the Flyer, clinging to Jez's rope.

'Where are we going?'

'To get Shy, my horse.'

'You got your own horse?'

'Yup.'

Unfastening the latch, I pulled back the horsebox door allowing sunlight to spill into the carriage. Then I swung inside.

Moonshine blinked at me. 'Will, but I thought folk weren't allowed to ride in the horsebox?'

'We're getting off at Pike's Ridge,' I announced, 'and the train don't stop so we'll have to fly.'

Jez swung inside to land beside me. 'Wow, ain't ever ridden a windhorse. She's a real beauty, pale as a mine wraith too!'

Shuddering at the thought of the

mine wraith I'd seen in the tunnel earlier, I noticed Moonshine eye the dwarf suspiciously. 'Who's this?'

'Jez. I met her on the roof of the Flyer,' I explained. 'She's coming too.'

'Talking to animals, you definitely got elf in you,' Jez grinned.

Moonshine looked slightly disgruntled at the idea of another passenger but didn't complain as we both got on the saddle. Trotting to the edge of the carriage, she leaped into the air.

'Weeeeeee!' Jez cooed loudly as we soared away from the steaming train.

'Easy with the hollering,' I said, shoving a finger in my ear, 'or I'll be half deaf time we get there.'

But Jez wasn't listening; instead she flung her arms out like wings. 'I'm a bird. I'm an eagle.'

'How about spitting some directions?' I cried.

Jez pointed. 'Over there!'

The ledge ran for quite some distance, chiselled out of the western arm of the West Rock. At its narrowest point there was barely room to walk.

At its widest point you could easily have placed a small house, not that that would have been a good idea as you would have walked out the front door to plummet miles down the rock face, landing with a splat in the middle of the Wastelands. Above and below there was jagged rock and smaller ledges, topped with mops of tangleweed and the twisted trees Jez had mentioned. It was towards the widest part that she now pointed.

'You OK to come down there, Shy?'

A loud whinny told me she was happy to try and, tilting her wings, she swooped down towards the ridge.

Landing, I dismounted before helping an open-mouthed Jez from the saddle.

'Reckon that was ten times more fun than riding the Flyer!' she gasped. 'Main ridge is that way,' she informed me. 'Have a look round if you want. I'll make us something to eat. I'm starving.'

I watched Jez deftly treading along quite a narrow ledge until she disappeared behind a bush of tangleweed. Then I led Moonshine across the ridge, a wave of disillusionment quickly rising in my chest.

'Jez was right,' I told Moonshine. 'Ain't nothing but a scorched rock and that grassy stuff.' I wondered if I had done the right thing getting off at Pike's Ridge. We'd probably have been in Deadrock by now if we'd stayed on the Flyer. I walked across the ledge kicking a stone, following its path as it skittered along the rock to disappear over the edge.

Moonshine tossed her head. 'What's that flag doing there?'

'What flag?'

'Over there.'

We made our way over to where something was jutting out of the ground up ahead. Kneeling to examine it, I discovered it was a tent peg, hammered into the rock with the tent long-blown over the edge, save for a torn piece of white material flapping in the breeze.

I gasped. 'This could be where Eldon was working. He'd probably have camped in a tent like this.'

Moonshine didn't answer; she was pawing the ground with her hoof. 'There's something here.' She kicked up some dust, but with it, a small shiny object.

I picked it up. 'A bullet case!' I choked back a tear, realising it might be a remnant from the shoot-out Pa was caught up in, maybe even from the bullet that had killed Pa? I pushed it down in my pocket. We looked around for a while but finding nothing else, I announced, 'Let's go back and see if Jez saw anything.'

A strong wind blew as we made our way back, following the route Jez had taken, where the ledge narrowed quite precariously. Up ahead I noticed a plume of smoke rising into the evening sky. We followed the smoke and came to a small flat clearing. A fire burned brightly between two boulders. Jez sat with a wooden spoon, stirring a pot of beans that bubbled on the flames. The aroma reminded me how hungry I was. I'd been too uptight to eat much of the breakfast Yenene had made that morning. I left Moonshine nibbling some tangleweed and took a seat on a log near the fire.

'You find what you were looking for?' Jez asked.

'Not really,' I shrugged. 'You recall an old elf camped on the ridge 'bout a year ago?'

She shook her head. 'Ain't been living here long as that. My ma only passed away around then.'

'You live here?'

'Sure do, and I tell you something, I wouldn't live anywhere else, not for a million gold pieces.' Jez smelled in a big lungful of air. 'I kinda discovered this place by accident. See I mainly work in the mine vents, keeping them free of quake debris and dust rat nests, anything that clogs 'em up, cutting off the flow of air to the main shafts.' She pointed towards a dark hole in the rock side. 'That vent leads all the way to the heart of the Deadrock Tin Mine.'

'Don't you worry that a tornado will sweep you over the edge? I mean, how do you sleep at night?'

'I didn't go to school but I ain't

stupid. I sleep on some straw just inside the vent.'

The sun began melting beneath the distant horizon. I shivered, feeling suddenly cooler. From the cover of rocks and logs came the rhythmic chirp of rock crickets, at times accompanied by the demented yelp of a moon coyote. Jez served the beans onto a tin plate and handed it to me with a hunk of bread.

'Thanks.'

'You're welcome, kinda nice to have company.'

After a few mouthfuls I asked, 'Where are you from?'

'I was born in the Wastelands, place called Oasis. You ever heard of it?'

I shook my head. 'No, nice name though.'

'After Ma and Pa died, I stayed with my crazy old aunt till I ran away and got me a job down the tin mine.'

'Couldn't you stay some place in Deadrock?'

'I couldn't live in Deadrock; hardly any dwarves live there. I tried it for a while but it didn't work out. Guess it's on account of where I come from. In the Wastelands there ain't a compass turn where you won't see horizon stretching for miles all around, playing tricks on your eyes, rippling the sand and rock like it were waves of the Far West Ocean.'

I liked the way Jez could paint a picture with her talk. I listened attentively, mopping up the bean juice with the bread.

'Out on the ridge here,' she went on, 'close your eyes with the wind blowin' in your face and you can be anywhere: the West Woods, Wastelands, anywhere. Ain't like Deadrock, that whole city's underground; it's suffocatin', chokes you like a noose.'

I ran a hand down my throat. I was sure I felt it tighten as Noose's ugly face swam through my head. 'That's where I'm headed.'

'As I told you, if you're smart you'll avoid it. Deadrock's an evil place.'

'I'm not staying, I got me some business there.'

'What sort of business?'

'I'm a bounty seeker!'

She looked me up and down. 'You mean a bounty slayer,' she snickered. 'Heck, you 'spect me to believe that?'

'I'm not bothered if you don't.'

'You sure don't look like a bounty slayer.'

'I said *seeker*. I don't plan on slaying anybody. Anyway, what's a bounty seeker s'posed to look like?'

'Well usually they ain't kids for starters.'

'I'm not a kid, I'm almost fourteen.'

'Well then a gun, now that's a biggy—all bounty slayers got themselves a gun, sometimes more than one.'

I reached inside my bag, noticing Jez shirk back and put a hand to the bone-handled knife in her belt.

'Guns aren't the elf way of things,' I said. 'And sometimes a gun isn't the best choice of weapon. They can draw attention where it's not wanted.'

Jez smiled. 'Draw, ha, I like that.'

I took out the blowgun. 'This is my gun.'

'Wow, it's beautiful.' Jez

83

examined the blowgun, running her stubby fingers over the carvings. 'Who you seeking?'

'Snake-bellied troll bandit name of Noose Wormworx. You ever heard of him?'

'Nope. He the one murdered your pa?'

'Yes.'

'Pretty brave going after a bandit, snake-belly too. My pa told me them trolls are the meanest, evilest folks on the rock. He said the only good snake-bellied troll is a dead one.'

'And my pa used to say that prairie dwarves are the kindest, hardest-working folks to come out of the Wastelands.'

'Reckon your pa was a very smart man.'

'He was.'

Taking out the sixberry pie Grandma had baked for Uncle Crazy Wolf, I broke it and shared it with Jez. I felt a bit guilty as it reminded me of the lie I'd told Grandma, saying I was going fishing, but there was no other way. Jez devoured it, saying it was the best pie

she'd ever eaten. I told her she could keep what was left as I guessed she hadn't tasted good pie for a long time.

When we'd finished, I noticed the darkening sky and stood up. 'Well, time we got going before it gets too dark to fly.'

'You're welcome to stay the night,' Jez offered. 'There's plenty of blankets. I gotta go to work for a bit but I'll be back soon enough.'

'Thanks, but I should be going. Maybe we'll bump into you on the way back up.' I glanced over the ridge. 'How far is it to Deadrock?'

'Ain't far,' Jez replied. 'You'll see the Deadeye tunnel round the bend in the rock face, the entrance to Deadrock's only a short flight from there.'

'Thank you for the beans.'

'You're welcome. Maybe see you again some day, next time you're on the run from whip-tails.' She grinned. 'Oh, an' thanks for the pie.'

Mounting Moonshine, I galloped off the edge of the ridge, out into open sky. When I glanced back, I saw the thin trail of smoke from the campfire spiralling upwards and Jez waving madly. Lifting my hat, I waved it back at her.

CHAPTER SIX

The Ghost of the Sky Cavalryman

We flew down the rock face, Shy's pale mane spilling out behind her, carefully following Jez's directions until we landed near a tunnel entrance. A wooden sign fixed above the tunnel read:

Disappearing into the gloomy passageway, I noticed that a narrow, gravel dirt path ran alongside the rail track just wide enough for a man on horseback, or a boy on horseback. I wondered if it would be total darkness all the way to Deadrock. Then there was the Flyer and the consequences of straying too close to the track to worry about.

'What's that light up ahead?' said Moonshine.

'Looks like a bunch of fireflies,' I replied, noticing an eerie purple glow up ahead.

Riding nearer to the glow I discovered that it wasn't fireflies. The strange radiance emanated from long stumps of wood, like branches, jutting from the walls at uneven intervals. Smaller shadows danced around each branch and, squinting through the gloom, I realised the shadows were from moth-like creatures obviously drawn to the light.

'What *is* that stuff?' asked Moonshine.

'Saddlewood,' I explained. 'We learned about at it school; branches of the saddlewood tree from the West Woods. When stripped of its bark the wood gives off a dull purple glow,

bright enough for trolls and goblins—
it's not seen much on the rock-top
towns.'

'Only time I've seen glowing wood is
when it's smouldering.'

'That's the twist, see,
you can hold a match to
saddlewood all day long if
you want to but it'll never
catch fire.'

We rode on silently for
a while, Moonshine's hoof
steps echoing in the long
murky tunnel.

'We need to talk about strategy,' I
said after a while. 'Y'know, for when
we get to Deadrock.'

'Great, er, but what's strategy?'

'Strategy's like how we're gonna
approach things.' I took out the wanted
poster of Noose and, stopping under a
glimmering saddlewood branch, leaned
forward to hold it to one side of her
face. 'Firstly, I want you to take a long
hard look at Noose's face cos when
we get to town we both gotta keep our
eyes peeled.'

'Four eyes are better than two, eh?'

said Moonshine, then she flinched. 'Ugh! Don't think I'd forget that ugly mug in a hurry.'

'I'd also appreciate it if you'd stay with me and not go wandering off. I'd guess it's gonna get quite gloomy. Oh, and no critter chatter unless I say it's all right, you got it?'

Moonshine gave a swish of her tail. 'Don't worry. You can count on me, I won't let you down.'

'I'm not grumbling, Shy, 's'just I gotta lay down some rules before we start the hunt proper. We don't know what's ahead of us and we might not get another chance to talk about stuff like this.'

Moonshine flicked her ears. 'I hear something. I think the Flyer's coming.'

We moved tight to the tunnel wall and moments later the Flyer stampeded past us, the noise doubled by the confined space, rattling my ribcage. Hardly daring to breathe, I clung to Moonshine's neck, feeling the tension in her muscles and smelling the familiar odour of her sweat. Seconds later the last carriage raced by in a blur of red paint and the Flyer was gone, leaving a trail of steam.

After a while the tunnel widened and a large cavern unfolded before us, lit by saddlewood branches; though instead of the usual purple hue, these branches glowed an eerie green colour. At first I thought we'd arrived in Deadrock but then I realised it was much too small and there were no buildings. Scouting the edges of the cavern, I discovered we'd stumbled upon an underground cemetery consisting of passages hewn out of the rock with rooms and recesses leading off them for burial chambers.

'What is this place?' asked Moonshine.

'A catacomb,' I announced with a shiver.

'A cata— what?'

'Graveyard.'

I noticed that some of the rooms had inscriptions carved on the rock but I couldn't make them out in the gloom. A few of the saddlewood torches were set lower in the cavern wall and reaching up, I freed a branch from its cavity. Then, dismounting, I held it near one of the inscriptions and read it aloud, a grin spreading over my face.

Big Joe

Entombed within
Lies Gabby Joe
His talk was fast
His draw was slow

'It's not funny. This place gives me the creeps,' said Moonshine. 'Can we get out of here?'

But my curiosity was getting the better of me, and I kept moving along the row of tombs reading the inscriptions.

Moonshine trotted to the end of the cavern. 'C'mon, I really think we should keep moving, I'd like to get out of this tunnel before the Flyer comes back.'

'Not scared are you, Shy?' I grinned.

Old Axle
Here lies
Ezekiel Axle
Aged 202
The good die young

I noticed some tools propped beside a freshly hewn tomb. There was no inscription. 'Reckon this here's a new tomb. Wonder what poor unfortunate will be checking in here?'

'Long as it's not us.'

I felt something scurry past me on the ground and held out the branch; dust rats, a family of big ones.

Moonshine was looking up at the cave roof. 'You see that?'

I walked over to join her. 'See what?'

'I'm sure I saw . . . naw couldn't have.'

'What? Saw what?'

'That pointy rock thing, I think it just moved.'

94

'A stalactite, which one?'

'That big one in the middle. Only, see, last time I looked it was over there and now it's . . .'

'Could be rock bats, or else your eyes are playing tricks on you.'

Moonshine blinked repeatedly. 'Maybe so.'

While we were staring at the cave roof, the stalactite broke off and fell to the cavern floor.

'Stalactites are fixed solid, they don't fall.' I moved closer and what I saw turned my guts. The stalactite was alive. Humming gleefully, rows of tiny little teeth were busily devouring the flesh of the fattest dust rat that had, seconds earlier, scurried past my feet. I felt a knot of bile rise in my throat.

'Look out!' cried Moonshine as another of the creatures fell, only narrowly missing my shoulder to fall, squirming, onto the ground, mouth gaping till with a guttural

complaint, it slithered back down the tunnel.

'What are they?' gasped Moonshine.

'Stykes,' said a voice. 'Better watch out too, one spears you and you're a gonner. It'll strip the flesh off your back in seconds.'

I spun round to see the shadowy figure of a cowboy sitting on a boulder in the middle of the tombs. 'W . . . Who are you?'

'Allow me to introduce myself.' The cowboy took off his hat but as he did so, his head wobbled ghoulishly on his shoulders. After a few wobbles it severed completely from his neck and rolled down his outstretched arm, where he caught it by a clump of grey hair. 'Headless Henk Holdem, though Henk'll do, thank you very much.' He grinned.

I felt the colour drain from my cheeks. For an awful moment I didn't know what to be more afraid of, the gruesome creatures or the ghostly stranger. I squinted. 'W . . . what are you? I can't see you clearly; it's like when you move I can see through you.'

'Probably clear enough,' Henk grinned. 'Being dead for a hundred years ain't done much for my complexion.' He looked at Moonshine, who seemed to have gone a shade paler. 'Fine horse you got there, boy.'

'She's a windhorse.'

'I'm dead not blind. I can see that all right—a thoroughbred too by the look of her.'

I nodded and Moonshine tossed her head proudly.

'Pardon me for askin' but what are you pokin' about down here for?'

'I wasn't poking about,' I replied. 'I'm headed for Deadrock.'

'Well you're headed the right way, though for you, reckon it could turn out to be the wrong way. What I mean is that maybe it ain't the sort o' place for a young cowboy like you.'

'Are . . . are you a spirit?' I asked, hesitantly.

'Heck no, I wish though,' the ghost gasped. 'Thanks for the compliment but I'm afraid that title's a little beyond ol' Henk.' He sighed, gazing skyward to where I was sure I spotted another styke skulking across the tunnel roof. 'Only good folks go up there, not good-for-nothings like me. No 'fraid I'm just a plain ol' wandering ghost, outlaw of the spirit world, if you like. Say, you gotta name, partner?'

'Will.'

'Pleased to meet you, Will.'

'I've never seen a ghost,' I remarked with a shudder.

'Most folks haven't. Everybody's too busy these days to notice us. Course another thing is that we tend to stay outta the way too.'

'That why you're down here?'

'Reckon it is. Deadrock's another favourite haunt o' mine, if you'll pardon the pun.' He sniggered.

I smiled. I figured Henk was probably the least scary ghost you could come across. Moonshine was nosing me, signalling me to keep moving but curious, I asked, 'Which tomb's yours?'

'C'mon, I'll show you.' Henk grinned. 'S'just a case of following the cobwebs—I'm in the oldest part of the graveyard.'

I followed Henk over to a gloomy corner where he pointed out a small tombstone. I held the torch near the inscription:

HENK
HOLDEM

PLAYING POKER
OL' HENK SAW RED
LOST HIS SHIRT
THEN LOST
HIS HEAD.

'What's it mean?'

'Happened over a hundred years ago.' He ran a finger across his throat. 'Day I'll never forget, of course.'

I gulped. 'I'm sure.'

'Not that a scoundrel like me deserved any better an ending. Just it came so sudden.' Henk grinned, then his expression changed to a more solemn one. 'In the old days gambling was banned. Why, if the sheriff caught you so much as tossing a coin in the air you could be locked up. Course that meant gambling still went on, only where the sky cavalry couldn't see it. Yup, snake poker went underground. Didn't take me long to track down a high-rolling game aboard an old train called the *Oretown Flyer*.'

I gasped. Pa had taken me to see it at the Oretown museum.

Henk went on. 'A group of ten or so men and a few goblins met when we could and played all day, as the train wound up and down the West Rock— till we lost or passed out from too much Boggart's Breath. Everything was fine and dandy till, one day, old crosspatch here gets himself into a fight, accusing a big lump of a man of cheating. In seconds the table's upturned and we're trading punches on the floor of the

101

caboose then . . .' he paused.

A faint whistle came from the darkness of the tunnel. I was captivated by the story. 'Then?'

'Then it turned nasty. The big lump drew on me, face like thunder. I'd never seen anyone turn like it. I knew he was serious. I tossed a chair at him and ran out, climbing a ladder onto the roof. Course the big lump climbed after me.'

Henk suddenly began floating away, out of the catacombs, back into the tunnel. I heard the faint noise of the Flyer.

'The big lump and me stumbled over the carriages. By this time I'd drawn my own six-shot blaster and we faced each other in a duel. The wind was howling like it is now, only then I could feel it on my face. Seemed like we stood frozen like that for ages, minds fuddled with whiskey, neither of us making so much as a thumb twitch to go for our guns. Then the big lump's face changed, warmed a bit, like he'd made a decision that maybe he didn't really want to be up on that windy roof. Me, I was too stubborn. I kept on facing him.

'Then he calls "Tunnel!" and I think, *I'm not falling for that old one*—I turn my head while he fills my belly full o' lead—no way. So I stare him right in the eyes, then the horror in them same eyes tell me he ain't lying.'

As Henk spoke, the Flyer suddenly appeared out of the gloom. I stifled an urge to cry out and warn Henk, who now stood on the track, then realised that the train couldn't harm him. I stared open-mouthed as Henk's ghostly, shimmering torso was engulfed by the cold metal of the Flyer.

Henk remained out of sight until the Flyer had passed. Then, head in his hands, eyes closed and a grave expression on his face, he floated over to me and said: 'Tunnel takes my head clean off and it's all over. I'm rising up—a ghost. The big lump is on his knees blubbering like a baby as my poor head's rolling along the carriage.'

I felt my heart race at the chilling tale. Closing my mouth, which had been gaping for most of the story, I swallowed hard. 'Figure that's the most terriblest thing I ever heard!'

'Terrible! Terrible!' yelled Henk, his eyes suddenly wild. 'Terrible!' He flung his head in the air, yelling as it spun round. 'I'll tell you what's *terrible* . . . I had a Snake Flush on the table in the caboose . . .'

I gazed round the gloomy cavern. 'So, are you stuck down here for good?'

Henk grinned. 'Us ghosts got different theories about that. A pal o' mine, Jake, thinks we're stuck down here as a punishment for something we did wrong when we were alive, so we're here for good. Course, he always looks

104

on the dismal side of things.'

'What do *you* think?'

'Me, I got a more positive outlook—I figure maybe it's cos there's something we still gotta do to earn our way up above, something good to sort of make up for all the mean stuff.' He screwed his face into a grimace then smiled.

'Like a second chance?'

'Something like that.'

Moonshine trotted out of the gloom and I took her by the reins. 'Been nice talking to you but I guess we should get going.'

'What takes you to Deadrock?'

'I got business with a snake-bellied troll named Noose Wormworx. Don't s'pose you've heard of him or . . . know where I could find him?'

The old ghost shook his hoary locks. 'Sorry, good luck to you anyway, and look after that fine horse of yours.'

'I will. Goodbye.'

CHAPTER SEVEN

Deadrock

We rode the remainder of the way to Deadrock in silence, treading a path away from the rail track. My thoughts were occupied with Henk and the gruesome stykes. If Yenene had told me creatures like that existed, I'd never have believed her, not to mention had nightmares about them. I wondered what other evil critters were native to the bowels of the Mid-Rock.

A succession of smaller chambers decorated with chalk drawings of pick-tooth wolves and bears finally led to the main chamber; a massive cavern topped by larger and more menacing stalactites, like suspended dagger blades bearing down. Some looked as though they would fall at any minute, to pierce the heart of the dim-lit town below.

As I stared I felt a chill run down my spine, imagining the slaughter if there were stykes that big.

The town lay nestled at the foot of a sloping cave wall overlooking a sea of stalagmites and twisting rail track. It consisted of tall, skinny wooden buildings, squashed together like organ pipes: a saloon, mercantile store, undertaker's, gunsmith, bank and the Deadrock Hotel. Hundreds of purple glowing saddlewood torches cast macabre shadows far up the cavern. I stared for a long time, mesmerised by the odd terrain. It was a chillingly magical place. A town I could never have imagined, not even in my wildest dreams. An invasion of smells battered my nose as we trotted closer. Damp, musty, smoky smells mostly but sometimes mingled faintly with familiar food smells; the smell of baking bread and sizzling sausages.

'This is it, Shy. Welcome to Deadrock!'

'This place is creepier than the graveyard,' she replied.

I rode Moonshine over the rocky ground, past the platform of Deadrock station and along a narrow road towards the overcrowded-looking town. I put up my collar to try and look inconspicuous among the mainly troll townsfolk, though I spotted a few tittering goblins roll out of the saloon and a hulking ogre blacksmith. I felt prickles run across my back and the hair on my neck stand up as I realised *Noose was here.* I had an almost magical sense of his presence. Maybe there was more elf in me than I gave myself credit for.

'Bread—get yer lovely fresh bread!'

I looked round to see a fat dwarf in a shop doorway. He had skin like tree-bark and wore a white apron. Jez had told me that dwarves were rare in Deadrock. She'd said few of them made the trip from the Wastelands, preferring the plains and open sky to rock and darkness. Dismounting, I was surprised to see that he was unusually tall. He was twice as wide as normal dwarves too.

The dwarf held out a loaf of bread to me. 'Hungry, partner? Freshest in Deadrock. Got something for that fine horse of yours too. Look like you could both use something.'

Moonshine's nostrils flared, as she smelled the tasty bread.

'I got business with a troll goes by the name of Noose Wormworx. Do you know if he's in town?'

The dwarf baker looked me up and down with black beady eyes. 'Wormwax,' he mispronounced. 'Never heard of him. You wanna buy some bread—fresh baked?'

It smelled delicious but I had to ration what little money I had. Licking my lips, I pointed to the two smallest loaves on the stall and pushed a coin into the dwarf's warty palm. 'Thank you.'

As I led Moonshine away, the dwarf called after us. 'You tried the saloon yet?'

'Not yet,' I called back.

'First place I'd visit if I was looking for someone. That is, if you can get in. They don't like kids much.'

'I'll keep my hood up.'

'You'll need to keep more than your hood up, keep your wits 'bout you too. There's a gunfight every other minute in that den.'

So far Deadrock hospitality seemed OK. Most folk painted a very black picture of the place, saying it was a gangster troll-hole—but was it? Here was a dwarf baker, plying his trade to earn an honest living—bread was tasty too. I figured if the different rock inhabitants could stop judging each other then there might just be a future for us all.

We journeyed on along the dusty street, past the mercantile store. A skinny, elfin-looking old man, clad from head to foot in black, carried some planks of wood inside the front door of the undertaker's. The windows were open and I could hear hammering coming from inside.

As we approached the saloon I noticed that the purple light emanating from the frosted-glass windows seemed bright by Deadrock standards as it spilled out onto the cobbled street. I tied Moonshine to a rail. 'Keep your eyes peeled, Shy, and whinny real loud if you see anything, y'hear?'

Moonshine nodded. 'Be careful, you heard what the dwarf said.'

I stopped outside and was summoning up the courage to enter when the sprung saloon doors scattered with a crash and two bodies, locked in a tussle, burst outside and fell into the dusty street, hats rolling with them. Fists and dust flew everywhere as a few curious onlookers gathered to watch. I used the distraction to duck under the nearest swinging door and slip inside.

The first thing I noticed, when my eyes adjusted to the bright, smoky atmosphere, was an upturned poker table and three trolls on their knees scurrying about like dust rats, picking up money that lay littered among the cards. I figured that snake poker should come with a sheriff's health warning.

I took a deep breath then, coughing

and spluttering from the pipe smoke, I strode up to the bar. A giant of a troll with arms like tree trunks, a swollen red face and flaring nostrils fixed two dark eyes on me. 'Ain't servin' ya, boy,' he growled, leaning towards me. As he did, I noticed something wriggle under his shirt. Could he be a snake-bellied troll? Probably. Slugmarsh and Jez said Deadrock was full of them. I felt an icy chill run up the back of my neck as I thought about the ghastly, slimy snakes that must be lurking under the garment.

'I don't want a drink,' I explained. 'Just some information.'

The bartender snorted, poured a shot of Boggart's Breath then skidded the glass along the bar top. Like a bullet, a green three-fingered hand shot out and grabbed it, sliding a coin back up along the counter.

'Gotta package for a Noose Wormworx. You know where I could find him?'

The troll poured another shot, drank it himself and slammed the glass back down. He belched loudly in my face. 'I want you to leave, boy.'

'Straight question deserves a straight answer.'

A fat she-troll wearing a pink frilled dress and enough lipstick to paint a barn wall leaned on the bar beside me. 'Lighten up, Punk, and give the boy a shot,' she drawled and clinked her empty glass against the bottle of Boggart's Breath.

'The boy ain't drinkin', he's leavin'.'

'Leaving! He just got here.' She embraced me with a burly arm. 'He's staying to watch the dancing!'

I shrugged, feeling my cheeks redden. 'S'OK, I'm not really keen on dancing.' Then I asked, 'Maybe you know where I could find Noose Wormworx?'

'Wormworx. Mighty fancy name, sounds rich,' she replied. 'Is he handsome? I'm looking for a rich, handsome man to take me away from this place. Actually, strike the handsome part, I ain't that fussy so long as he's rich.'

'He's an outlaw and a cold-blooded killer.'

She whirled round, flouncing off in the direction of the stage. 'Fooooooey! Had my fill o' that type—gotta go, my stage is calling me.'

Suddenly the saloon doors flew open. The tinkling piano music stopped abruptly. A mean-looking snake-bellied troll with a bloody nose stood holding open the swinging doors. I recognised him as one of the trolls from the street

brawl. The corner of his lip twitched and he scowled over in the direction of the poker table.

I felt myself being dragged backwards and upwards over the bar counter. It was only when I was underneath it that I realised the bartender had grabbed me and was now crouched beside me, a strange detached look on his face. Seconds

later, deafening gunfire erupted through the saloon. I peered through a crack in the wooden counter and saw the poker table topple over onto its side and a gun appear over the top, firing back at the troll. The troll wobbled in the doorway clutching his belly then fell over. There was a long silence. I held my breath, not taking my eye away from the crack, and noticed the saloon doors open again and the elfin undertaker enter, shuffling over to crouch by the body. Reaching in his pocket, he took out what looked like a measuring tape and busily began measuring the unfortunate gunfighter. When he'd finished he dragged the troll by the legs out of the saloon, shaking his head and tut-tutting.

The bartender got to his feet, lifting up the bar flap. 'Go, or I'll throw you out.'

I didn't hesitate. I walked round to the other side of the counter but felt a bony hand grab me as I tried to leave.

'Couldn't help overhearing,' rasped an old troll sucking a gnarled pipe. He looked drunk and kept blinking,

116

struggling to focus his blood-shot eyes. 'But I knows where you can find this Noose critter you're looking for.' He tapped a finger on his squat purple-veined nose. 'If you're interested. S'just that information don't come cheap round these parts.'

I rummaged in my bag. 'I don't have much but I'd appreciate your help.' I placed a coin in the wrinkled palm.

The troll bit down hard on it with a black tooth. He looked both ways, nodding for me to come closer. 'Passed him on the edge o' town only tonight,' he whispered.

'Which side o' town?'

'Past the hotel, where the road narrows, hanging about with a bunch o' nobodies.'

I stifled a cough at the stench of the old troll's filthy clothes. Then, tipping my hat, I made my way across the glass-strewn saloon.

Out in the street, Moonshine was head to head arguing with a fierce-looking, wingless black stallion.

'Smell funny, huh? Well now I know you're from outta town,' growled the stallion.

'Sure ain't from *this* town,' Moonshine hissed.

'You got something against this town? Cos if you have then I can arrange for you to leave it right now!'

'Oh yeah, you gonna make me? I gotta warn you that my pa was in the sky cavalry, y'know.'

'That's enough, Shy,' I broke in quickly, untying the reins and leading her off down the street.

'We can't be getting into squabbles,' I chided. 'You forget about the strategy?'

'He started it,' she huffed.

'We've got to keep us a low profile in town. Not draw attention to ourselves, now c'mon.'

Moonshine agreed, though I still caught her flicking her tail in the stallion's direction. 'Where are we going?' she asked.

'A smelly old troll from the saloon says he saw Noose up on the edge of town.'

I mounted her, then set out along the dim-lit street, squinting at the signs on the various buildings and inspecting every troll in case he might be Noose. At the end of a row of buildings the road narrowed and the light grew dimmer.

'The old troll must've been talking about round here somewhere.'

Dismounting, I wandered out into the middle of the road and almost walked into the towering wooden gallows. A lump swelled in my throat as I surveyed the swinging noose. *Noose!* Suddenly, it dawned on me. The old troll had said he'd seen Noose hanging about with a bunch of nobodies— well he was right, here was a hangman's noose and there was nobody about. He'd tricked me! I should've been mad but, staring up at the deadly circle of rope, I couldn't help but chuckle.

I was still staring up at that noose when I heard heavy footsteps,

then laden breathing getting closer . . . closer. The next thing I was on the ground, a rifle barrel in my face. It was the dwarf baker I'd met earlier. 'Did you think you could steal my purse and get away with it?' he snarled.

'Don't shoot! I didn't steal your purse.'

'Liar! Hand it over or you're dead!'

I quickly decided that maybe my first impressions of Deadrock townsfolk had been wrong.

The dwarf prodded my chest with the rifle. 'Get a move on, turn out your bag and pockets!'

'It wasn't me. I swear!' I pleaded.

With a loud neigh, Moonshine skittered sideways, arching her neck to square up to the dwarf who swung the rifle at her. 'No heroics now, horse!'

'Shy, back off, I'll handle it.' I emptied what little money I had from my pocket and the dwarf took it.

'Where's the rest of it? Open the bag!'

I opened the bag. 'Bread, that's all I got. I swear.'

'Sneak thief. You've stashed it, ya

horrid little parasite!' And he brought the rifle butt across my face. I heard the noise of the crack and felt a sharp stinging pain, then nothing more.

*   *   *

I came to—couldn't have been much later—and I was lying on the spot where the troll had hit me.

'Shy,' I croaked wearily, nursing the bruise on my head. She was nowhere to be seen.

I heard footsteps nearby and my eyes slowly focused on a figure skulking in the gloom, edging closer. The mystery figure, too thin to be the dwarf baker, reached out a hand, making a grab for the bag that had been tossed by my side. I grabbed the strap as it ascended into the air. But the blow had sapped my strength. It was a young troll; I heard him curse as he yanked the bag from my grip.

Suddenly I was wide awake. The bag had everything in it, the poison, the blowgun. Without it the hunt was over. It was back to Oretown to try and

121

explain to Grandma why I didn't have her gutfish. Summoning my last ounce of strength, I swung out a foot in the direction of the troll's legs, sending him tumbling over the ground. A leather purse fell from his coat with a noise like jangling money—stolen dwarf baker money, I guessed. The troll began to crawl across the ground when a pair of hooves hit him square on the back, sending him tumbling again.

I pinned him to the floor by his arms and took back the bag. 'Nice work, Shy. Where'd you get to?'

'That baker tried to steal me,' she said, bringing her rump sharply up in a bucking gesture, 'till I unseated him; bigger they are the harder they fall!'

'Get off me, elf scum,' seethed the stranger and he spat in my face.

I was growing tired of being insulted, especially by a troll younger than myself. 'I don't think we're much different from one another, except maybe that I'm not a common sneak thief.' I drew a dart from the bag and jabbed it under his throat.

'Tipped with poison,' I bluffed;

there was no way I could start fiddling with jar lids but I could pretend. 'Goes straight to the nervous system and shuts it down . . . agonising end.'

'Please. I was hungry . . . I . . .'

'I'm hungry myself but I'm not robbing folks.'

'W . . . who are you, stranger?'

'No concern of yours. You lived here all your life?'

Trembling, the young troll nodded. 'Why?'

'I'm looking for somebody, outlaw by the name of Noose Wormworx. You heard of him?' I thrust the dart harder against the troll's warty flesh.

'Uh uh,' the troll answered through clenched teeth for fear of the dart piercing his throat.

'I don't believe you.' I was growing more and more irritable. 'I can't believe that no one in this whole spirit-forsaken town has heard of one of the biggest troll bandits on the rock.' Then I had an idea. Screwing up my face in the meanest grimace I could muster, I drew back the dart as though to finish the troll off.

His nostrils flared in cold terror. 'Wait!'

Slowly, I brought the dart back to rest under the troll's chin. 'I'm listening.'

'Swear I ain't heard of a critter called Wormworx,' he gasped, 'but . . . but there's a snake-belly troll goes by the name of Noose over at the tin mine. Caught me thievin' a while back—beat me black and blue.'

'What'd he look like?'

'Ugly critter . . . big warty nose. Fists like boulders too; bloodied my nose real bad.'

'Where's this tin mine?'

'Just outta town, near the freight station, but you won't get near it. The guard shoots trespassers like he was shooting dust rats.'

I released my captive. Though I realised it could be a tissue of lies to buy his life, the thief's story was the first real lead I'd had and this troll kid wasn't worth wasting good poison on.

'G'on get lost!' I chased the boy into the darkness. Then I slowed, feeling my legs stagger under me. My head pounded from the earlier rifle blow and I felt giddy. The ground seemed to tremble and I felt like I was sinking. Blinking, I looked round to see if Moonshine was following me. It seemed darker here, very dark. The next thing, everything went black.

CHAPTER EIGHT

Snake Poker

'Will! Willlll!'

I grabbed the gutfish by the tail as it danced on the end of the rod. Who was there? No folk lived here, not in this wilderness.

'Will, can you hear me?'

I called out across the river. 'I'm keeping this one for Grandma.' I opened my eyes. A face swam above me.

'Keeping what for Grandma?' the face asked.

I struggled to focus; a task made harder by the fact that the face was an apparition. The face was Henk's.

'What the heck happened to you? You were out cold; you even slept through a rock quake.'

I realised I was still lying in the narrow street on the edge of town. And that the gutfish was my bag strap. 'Case of mistaken identity,' I groaned.

'Where's my horse?'

'She's right here. Who hit you?'

'Fat dwarf with the butt of his rifle, though felt like the Flyer at full steam.'

'So this is what you call business? Y'know, I'm finding you more curious by the minute, kid.'

I shot him a testy glance. 'A small setback.' Shakily, I got to my feet then lifted the bag over my shoulder and put on my hat. I glanced round and saw that one of the buildings on the edge of town had completely collapsed during the rock quake I'd slept through, and a group of trolls was pulling a groaning figure from the rubble.

'Woah there, you're as wobbly as a newborn foal.' Henk rubbed the ghostly white stubble on his chin. 'You sure you ain't in some kind of trouble? Cos I'd only be too—'

'It's nothing I can't handle.' I walked over and gently stroked Moonshine's nose.

She lowered her head and spoke softly. 'Are you OK?' But I put a finger to her lips.

'No need to hush her.' Henk smiled.

'Critter chatter's fine with me. Can't understand why they make such a hullabaloo about it. Besides, while you were snoozing, me and Moonshine here had time to get acquainted.'

'You can critter chatter?' I grinned. 'How come?'

'Surprised me too, when I found out I could do it years ago. I guess it's a ghost thing. It's like I'm more tuned into nature, especially animals. Turns out we share a few mutual interests, ain't that right, Moonshine?'

'Henk was in the sky cavalry,' said Moonshine excitedly.

'For less than a year till they booted me out for always being late for duty, that's if I even bothered to show up at all,' he added, hanging his head so low that it tumbled off his neck. He caught it, cradling it in his hands. 'Biggest mistake I ever made when I was alive and one I regret to this day. Sky cavalry would have made a soldier, not to mention a man, out of me—instead of the waste o' skin I turned into.'

I took Moonshine's reins and started out along the road. 'We gotta go.'

128

'Where you headed?'

'Tin mine.'

Henk followed. 'I'm headed that way too. I'll walk with you. There's a big game tonight over at Deadrock freight station.' He pointed to the dilapidated old building located behind a small platform on the other side of town.

'Game?'

'Snake poker—few ghost pals of mine from way back.' He grinned. 'Old habits die hard, if you'll pardon the pun.'

The snake-poker game I'd seen back at the saloon, and the shoot out, flashed through my mind—snake poker sure was a deadly game.

'Then you're not following me?' I said.

Henk looked taken aback. 'Following you? Heck, no. Confess to being a mite concerned, 'specially as one minute you're strolling round tombstones and the next brawlin' with dwarves.' He wrung his hands together. 'No. Once a month the boys meet for

129

a high-rolling game of snake poker. You're welcome to join us.' He pointed to my black eye. 'It's safer out o' town and you can tether Moonshine without having to worry about her being stolen.'

I shook my head, feeling it throb. 'I can't, I got . . .'

Henk held up two ghostly palms. 'I know . . . business.'

Up ahead, the road, which was really just part of the cave floor that had been cleared of stalagmites, split in two. One road followed the rail track towards the freight station, while the other led to the tin mine at the edge of Deadrock.

'Guess I'll be on my way. Look after yourself and that fine horse,' said Henk. 'If you change your mind, you know where to find me.'

I touched the brim of my hat. 'Yeah, see ya.'

Expectantly, I mounted Moonshine and followed the road round to the mine.

'S'pose he just happened to appear out of nowhere?' I commented as we rode.

'Yeah, he said he was just passing.'

'Asks a lot of questions.' I chewed my bottom lip. 'Maybe it'd be best if we play our cards close to our chests.'

'I like him.'

'I'm not saying I don't like him, 's'just I don't want anyone following us around.'

As we rode nearer, I caught sight of a huge wooden sign above the dark, gaping mouth of the mine. It read:

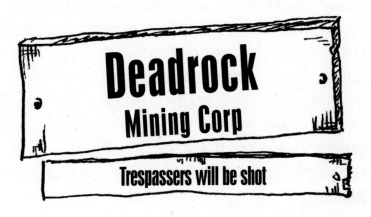

I felt my throat tighten and I swallowed a lump. Spiky wooden fencing formed the boundary of the mine and prevented me from getting as close as I'd have liked.

'You up for riding a trail through those stalagmites, Shy?'

131

'Can't we just fly over them?'

'Draw attention to ourselves. Besides, some of those stalactites are pretty low.'

She blew air heavily out of her nostrils. 'Guess so then, just hope they ain't got teeth!'

Heading off the main track, we weaved a precarious route through the stalagmites and uneven ground to a spot that was facing, and close to, the mine entrance. A thick saddlewood stump on one side of the cave mouth lit the surroundings but still, this far from town, it was very gloomy.

Two burly trolls appeared and began pulling open skull-topped iron gates laced with barbed wire, as a line of dark figures lumbered out of the gloom.

Troll miners. Bowed and broken-looking, they filed out of the mine entrance. On their squat heads they wore hard hats. In blackened hands they carried pickaxes and spades, hammers and wedges, buckets and saddlewood lamps. Most of them were coughing and hacking. The trolls pulling open the gates, cursed at them to hurry up.

'Move along there,' shouted one, gruffly, cracking a whip at the feet of a stout troll.

'Still your lash, Ax, bin a long hard day.'

'And you're making it longer with your dawdlin', Hegg Grumill, now move along!'

A fat, horned troll appeared leading a mine horse out of the gloom, and I gasped. It was barely recognisable as a horse. Not like the winged mustangs and chestnuts of the Gallows's ranch that I had grown up with. This horse's head was bowed low, face downbeat and eyes lifeless, like the troll miners's. Its coat of black and silver was unhealthy. *Probably through ill-feeding*, I mused. It was pulling a heavy cartful of ore that looked far too full for one animal.

Lastly, two trolls struggled to carry a stretcher out of the mine; on it lay a lifeless troll, flat on his back. His mouth gaped open and his eyes bulged, frozen in a look of pure terror that made my blood run ice cold. 'Mine wraith got this one, Ax,' they informed the troll with the whip.

'Pity. He was a good worker.'

When the line of miners had dispersed into the gloom, the burly trolls secured the gates and stood guard outside, shouldering enormous rifles.

Moonshine snorted, then asked, 'What are you thinking?'

'I'm thinking we're not gonna get anywhere near that mine tonight.'

'Didn't Jez say she works down the mine?'

'Been thinking about that,' I said. 'She'd never heard of Noose, though. Still, might be worth a visit to see if she can get us inside.'

'Let's go.'

'It'll be too dark outside for flyin', and Grandma says dragons sometimes hunt at night around the lower western arm. We'll go first thing in the morning.'

My head still pounded from the blow as I gently tugged the reins and turned Moonshine round. For the first time I felt deeply disheartened. I wondered what I thought I could do. How would I ever get near such a place? And even if I did somehow manage to get inside, would I ever get out alive? One thing was certain—my hunt was over for the day. The troll thief was right; the mine was a fortress and the guards looked extremely trigger-happy.

A sudden tiredness gripped me. It had been a long day. I rode slowly back along the path to town to try and find somewhere safe to stay—if there was such a place in Deadrock. I figured Moonshine must be just as tired after the long journey from Oretown, though she'd be too stubborn to admit it.

As we passed the freight station, a faint light in the small window got the better of my curiosity and I took the short road to the platform. Riding round the back, I dismounted near a trough filled with fresh water and while Moonshine drank, I stood on a barrel to peer through the window. To my surprise, I saw a group of bearded ghostly figures wearing cowboy hats, pale and shimmering like Henk, sitting

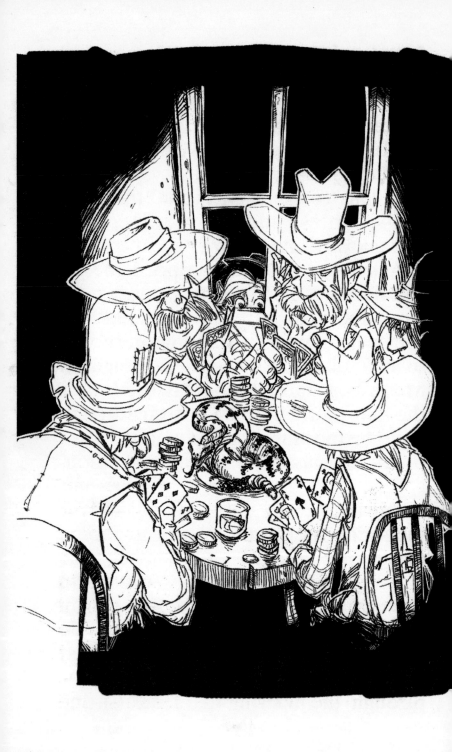

round a table. They were playing cards. It was an odd sight as the cards, which were real, were being held by unreal fingers, and at times appeared to float by themselves. In the centre of the table, coiled tightly like a piece of luminous green rope, was the rare and magical rock snake.

Back at Phoenix Creek I'd watched the sky cowboys and ranch hands play snake poker and knew that during a game the snake was trained to enter a mystical trance, gazing round the table of players with huge eyes, probing their minds for weakness, a glimmer of a thought. If the snake detected a bluffer then it would strike, putting that player out of the game.

The snake seemed to notice me, arching its thin neck and directing menacing eyes that glowed yellow at me.

'What's he looking at?' I overheard one of the ghosts say. The ghost opposite him got up and paced to the window. Leaping off the barrel, I ducked behind it just as a head came through the wall of the building and looked around.

'Don't see nothin',' said the ghost, and disappeared inside again.

I sat on the edge of the raised platform, legs dangling while Moonshine nosed at the ground, foraging hopelessly for a juicy clump of grass. I took the wanted poster from my bag. My head ached and my vision blurred and, for a moment, two Nooses scowled up at me from the paper. I gazed over at the tin mine. Snakes lived under rocks so it seemed a fitting hiding place for low-belly scum like Noose.

'Hadn't figured you for a bounty slayer,' said a voice behind me.

'Wha . . .?' I turned round to see Henk gawping over my shoulder. 'You always go around sneaking up on folk?'

Henk grinned. 'Ain't that what ghosts do? Boo and all that?'

'So now you know what I'm here for, you sure you haven't seen or heard of him?'

Henk shook his head, studying the poster. 'Ugly-looking critter—what'd he do?'

Wanted
DEAD OR ALIVE

Noose Wormworx
GENEROUS REWARD

I answered him through clenched teeth. 'Killed my pa.'

Henk gasped. 'Your pa? What happened?'

'Shoot out. Pa had Noose in his sights; he shouted for cover but . . . well it wasn't there.'

'I'm sorry.'

I frowned. 'Pa didn't think. He shouldn't o' relied on cover, should've waited an' took him out when he'd a clean shot. S'why I'm riding out after Noose, alone.'

Henk sighed. 'Your pa done nothing

wrong trusting others. Sometimes there ain't time to think. He made a call, took a chance, and taking a chance comes hand in hand with responsibility.'

After a pause Henk added: 'None of my business but exactly how long do you expect to live walking around Deadrock with a poster of an outlaw in your pocket?'

'Long enough,' I answered testily, rolling up the poster.

'You figure this Noose critter's down the tin mine?'

'Gotta lead he might be hiding out there, but it's closed up for the night.'

'Guess that's where I'd go if I was on the run from the law. You know, if you're looking for a partner to help you track him down . . .'

'You?'

'Sure, why not? You could do a lot worse than having a ghost around. We can sneak up on folk, not to mention walk through walls. Can take a rifle bullet too.'

'Thanks, but like I said . . . I work alone.'

Moonshine snorted in protest till I added, 'Just me and Shy.'

'Suit yourself, kid, but it's a big old rock,' Henk said reflectively, 'and life can be a long trail for you to travel it alone all the time.'

'Prefer it that way.'

'Well, 's'your call, but at least lose the poster.'

'Like you lost your shirt again, huh?' I said, remembering the inscription on Henk's tomb.

'What?'

'The big game, how come you ain't playing?'

'Oh, didn't I mention? I only come to watch.'

I stuffed the poster in the bag. 'How come? Thought you loved snake poker.'

'Hand me that axe down there.'

I lifted the heavy axe and passed it to Henk's outstretched hand. It passed clean through it, falling to the ground.

'Call it a penance, nothing less than I deserve,' Henk explained. 'See, most ghosts can learn to hold stuff, after a time of course, but me—can't hardly hold my tongue.'

I sniggered but Henk's eyes looked solemn. 'Is there nothing you can do?'

'Too late. My own selfish living is the cause and I can't turn back the clock.' Henk shimmered in the dim light like he was shivering, then he got to his feet. 'Come and meet the boys.'

I pushed my fringe up into my hat. 'No thanks, I should find somewhere to stay.'

'No need. Stay here. Plenty o' nice comfy hay bales inside, and your horse'll be safe out here. Oh, and I promise we'll not disturb you on account of us ghosts not sleeping and all that.'

'Guess I could crash here till the mine opens,' I said. Truth was, I was beat and had no idea where else to stay. And it would be kind of nice to have company—even though they were all dead. 'I'd appreciate it if you don't tell anyone what I'm doing in town.'

'Got my word.'

I stroked Moonshine's nose then followed Henk into the freight store. Bags of what looked like grain lay stacked all around the inside, with the table in the middle. None of the ghosts looked up as I approached.

After making a loud throat-clearing noise, Henk introduced me to the company. 'Boys this here's Will, a real live 'un friend o' mine.' No one budged. 'Elf kid from up the rock.'

A meaty-faced ghost raised an eye then tipped his hat. 'Pleased to meet ya.'

'Howdy,' said the downbeat next to him, running a hand through waist-length grey locks of greasy hair.

'I'm picking you off, you're bluffing!' a toothless spectre grunted.

'Gonna cost ya to find out.' The ghost grinned, pulling his cards closer to his chest.

'Call!'

The players revealed their cards and the toothless spectre rubbed his hands gleefully then, reaching out an arm, scooped the pot towards him.

Henk addressed the new winner. 'Not gonna say howdy to the boy, Jake?'

I wasn't sure who hissed louder, Jake

or the snake.

'Case you hadn't noticed, we're in the middle of a poker game here,' Jake drawled, 'so unless the Great Spirit has seen fit to give you back your ghost grip and you wanna play, then shut your mouth!'

Henk grinned. 'Snake poker always makes him grouchy.'

I pulled a box over and sat down to watch the game. I recognised the old coins the ghosts were gambling with. They weren't in use anymore but Yenene kept a collection in her room and I would sometimes shine them with a rag and some root vinegar. I fished a coin from my pocket and shoved it in the middle of the table.

'Live 'uns ain't allowed to play,' Jake snapped.

But I was ready for him. 'I'm playing for Henk.'

Henk raised an eyebrow then sat on a barrel behind me. 'You boys ain't gotta problem with that, have you?'

The ghosts shook their heads. 'Ain't seen a kid o' your sort round here before. You livin' in town?' said one

144

of them. I detected a sudden growing curiosity in me.

'Nope. I'm looking for work . . . in the tin mine,' I replied.

All the ghosts except Jake looked up.

'Pretty crazy,' said the long-haired one as he dealt another hand. 'Jake, you worked for old Klondex, didn't ya?'

Jake growled. 'That mine's nothing but a death trap. Do yourself a big favour, kid, and take the train back outta here first thing in the morning.'

I gasped. 'You worked down the mine?'

'Not the tin mine, the deep mines. It were all different then.'

'Never heard of the deep mines,' I said.

'You wouldn't have. This were a hundred years ago, before it closed. Troll name of Zeb Klondex owned it in them days and it weren't tin we were pulling from the rock—it were gold; big chunks of it, like blocks of Mid-Rock City cheese. Till the High Sheriff closed it down.'

'Why'd he close it?'

'Geological reasons. Something

about weakening the rock. Miners were getting killed every week in the rock slides. That and the gold getting harder to find. Figured it weren't worth it for the loss of life and threat o' the western arm crumbling into the Wastelands. Now, can we get on with the game?'

'Weren't there something about him not leaving and the sheriff's men burying him with the gold?' Henk queried.

Jake nodded. 'Rumour has it old Zeb fought the decision to close the mine till the bitter end. Said he wouldn't leave—and he didn't. The whole place came in round him during a rock quake as they were sealing the mine for good.'

The snake suddenly struck at the long-haired ghost and he tossed in his cards to roars of laughter from the others. 'Low-down reptile—I'm out!'

My hand was poor. Face up I had a Six of Bullets, a Four of Eagles and a Nine of Bats. A dead-man's hand, I'd heard the ranch hands call it as it was usually a bluffer's hand, and in the old days players had used poisonous snakes.

Poker-faced, I shoved in two coins. 'I'm in.' But I was still pondering something.

'How do you know they're not mining gold in there now?'

Jake stared at the snake. 'Like I said, place was all sealed off over fifty years ago. The High Sheriff of the West Rock ordered his top officers in the sky cavalry to keep a close eye on it, with regular inspections and all that. Now, can we cut the history lesson, I need to concentrate!'

Henk grinned. 'You're just sore that all this conversation's stopping the snake getting inside the boy's mind.'

The snake reared its head at me like it was going to strike.

'Spirits help us, keep talking, kid,' gasped Henk.

Jake licked his lips, sensing another victory, when I suggested coolly: 'If I'm not mistaken, a player can drop a dead-man's hand and get a new hand once every sitting—Oretown rules!'

A sudden hush fell over the table. Even the snake froze.

Henk rubbed his chin. 'A big drop, heck you're right, kid.'

The long-haired one nodded. 'Kid knows his snake poker.'

Face reddening, Jake puckered up his mouth. 'We don't play Oretown rules.'

'We don't play Jake rules either,' said Henk. 'And rules is rules, no matter what their origin.'

Fuming, Jake put my cards to the bottom of the deck and dealt me a fresh hand. A grin slithered its way across Henk's mouth as they were dealt. Dragon of Hearts, Snake of Arrows and a Dragon of Stars—mostly myth cards, much better than our first hand, though to be any good we needed more of the same. I thumbed at my face-down cards as the snake let out a loud hiss, coiling round to fix Jake with a stare. I was sure I saw ghost sweat on Jake's forehead.

Gritting his teeth, Jake shoved in all his coins and cried. 'Call!'

Grinning round at Henk, I set my cards on top of the others. 'House of Dragons.'

Furiously Jake threw his cards on the table. 'What magic is that elf kid using? You're a four-flushing cheat, kid, talking 'bout the mine as a decoy while you pull cards from your sleeve.'

Henk got to his feet. 'You take that back, Jake. The boy won fair and square!'

I leaned forward to collect the pot but paused, feeling dizzy and a bit sick. I felt the bruise on my head and winced.

'Oretown rules, my foot,' Jake complained. 'Never even heard of them.'

'Boy's been clubbed by a dwarf,' Henk barked. 'He don't wanna listen to you hollerin' on, making his head worse. You all right, boy? You've gone a funny colour.'

'Head's thumping like a Gung-Choux battle drum.'

'Why don't you turn in? There's a

149

straw bale over in the corner.'

'Maybe I will, though I'll take it outside and sleep with Shy.'

Carrying the hay out to where Moonshine lay, I curled up beside her, feeling her warmth on my skin. She blew gently out her nostrils and moved a wing to cover me.

'Goodnight,' she breathed.

'S'always night in Deadrock,' I replied wearily, kicking off my boots. 'Though I'm not so sure about the good.'

CHAPTER NINE

The Mine Wraith

I woke the next morning—at least I figured it was morning—to find my head felt a bit better. The swelling was down, though it was still tender to touch. Moonshine was already up and drinking at the trough. I wandered inside the freight station.

The first thing to strike me was the silence. Only sheer exhaustion had helped me get to sleep last night over the noise of the poker party and the strange surroundings. Where were they all? Haunting? Henk, I figured, had probably gone back to the catacombs. I was glad. It meant I could get on with my plan without any fuss.

Some bread sat by my hat and I devoured it hungrily, thinking about Noose. He was all I really thought about lately. Would today be the day I found him down the mine? A

151

gut feeling told me I was close. I kept some bread for Moonshine and was searching for the bag to put it in when I froze. It was gone. I heard the whistle of the Flyer and raced outside.

Two railroad men were loading boxes and barrels aboard the freight carriage of the train.

'Howdy! Figured you were gonna sleep all day,' Henk called from the back of the caboose. 'I'm hitchin' a ride to the catacombs. Come with me, you can read some more of the tomb inscriptions.'

Spotting my bag on top of one of the freight boxes (I remembered setting it there last night when the box had been inside the freight store), I hurried over to quickly grab it. 'I'll pass thanks.'

'Must be something mighty important in that bag. You seem pretty anxious about it,' Henk grinned. Then with a wink he added, 'You sure you don't need a partner?'

'I gotta do this alone—better that way.' The carriage began to move away and I turned back. 'But thanks, huh?'

'Sure thing, li'l deputy. You take

care now.' Henk waved. 'Oh, nearly forgot, the boys wanted me to pass on their thanks for last night. Said the look on Jake's face when he saw that House of Dragons was worth a big fat Klondex gold nugget. Even ol' Jake saw the funny side, later on. Oh an' he left you some bread.'

'I got it, tell him thanks.'

I smiled and walked over to get Moonshine. 'Got us a big day today, Shy. We'll fly up to Pike's Ridge to find Jez; see if she can somehow get us inside the tin mine. Don't fancy our chances much against those troll guards.' I gave her the bread and she almost swallowed it whole.

We started out on the road back to the tin mine. Opening the bag, I took out the wanted poster and tore it up, scattering the pieces as we rode the same route through the stalagmites to a spot facing the mine entrance. Henk was right, it was foolish carrying it about.

My throat tightened again as I saw the sign in the distance still proclaiming that trespassers would be shot. Then I gasped, hardly able to believe my luck. The troll guard was sitting on a boulder by the main entrance, head drooped in a deep sleep. And the menacing, skull-topped gates were wide open. *So much for mine security*, I thought.

Telling Moonshine to stay back, I crouched low and picked my way carefully through the stalagmites towards the mine. Pausing for breath near the gaping chasm, I had a strange feeling something wasn't quite right. The pallor of the troll's grey, warty skin seemed unusually pale, its fat belly, criss-crossed with studded bullet belts, oddly still.

Slowly I crept closer, only a horse's-length away from the guard. A bat swooped out of the mine and I ducked to avoid it. I glanced over at the guard, only to see him slide sideways off the boulder, collapsing in a heap on his belly. And that's when I saw it. Embedded in the guard's back was a tapered piece of what looked like stone.

I waved for Moonshine to come and, trotting up beside me, she shuddered. 'That what I think it is sticking outta him?'

'Reckon it's a styke, all right.' I moved closer and saw the creature had burrowed right through the guard's coat and was hungrily devouring the troll's flesh.

Repulsed, I stared, hearing my every breath. Part of me wanted to walk the other way, back to the station, to follow Henk out to the catacombs or further, back to Oretown. But the prospect of finding Noose was roping me in. And the dead troll had given me an idea. The troll's coat, even though it had a hole in it, could buy me some time to look round the mine, undercover.

I took out the blowgun, aiming at the thicker end of the styke's tapering body. With a soft whistle, the dart buried deep into the creature's flesh. I watched as, in a few moments, it lost its rigidity, flopping onto the troll's back, though its mouthparts still held the troll's flesh in a vice-like grip. Grasping its slimy body, I ripped it off, tossing it on the ground. Then I removed the coat and put it on. It was far too big for me but that was all the better; more for me to hide under. A blanket lay draped across the boulder the troll had sat on and I removed it, draping it over Moonshine, covering her wings. The next thing, I rubbed my hands in the dirt of the mine floor and began running them over Moonshine's shoulders and back.

'What are you doing?'

'You're too clean for a mine horse and too healthy. Try to bow your head and look miserable like the others.'

Blackening my own face, I led Moonshine into the mine. We kept to the narrow gauge track that ran down the middle; it was easier to walk on, especially in the poor light.

After a while, a noise up ahead prompted me to move closer to the walls. A faint smell of smoke reminded me of the saloon.

Staggering through a darker patch, fear gripped me as I couldn't see the roof to check for stykes. I felt my way with my hands, moving them over the damp craggy rock. The next thing I felt something grab my wrist.

'Gotcha!' said a deep voice. I cried out as I was pulled into a small, dim-lit alcove off the main shaft. An ugly big troll mouth blew pipe smoke in my face. I froze with fear as two more trolls clustered round me.

They were a grisly bunch. Dressed from head to foot in black bark cloth, they stank of sweat and bacca-weed smoke. Their faces were black too, and bulbous wart-covered noses stuck out below beady eyes—eyes that regarded me warily.

'Look what's snooping about,' said one of them.

'He's a bit on the short side for a guard, I reckon.'

'Looks like a human kid.'

'Naw, not with ears like that. Got some stinkin' rotten elf blood in 'im, I'd say.'

The biggest troll pulled some equipment out of the last of a row of carts. 'Ax don't allow intruders sneaking about,' he snarled.

'Might figure yuh gotta mind on

157

stealin' ore.'

'I'm not stealing. I'm looking for work. The guard let me in,' I fibbed, 'before a styke dropped on him, killing him.' I fought to keep calm, to think. Think a way through this.

The big troll fingered the sleeves of the coat I wore. 'Ain't thievin', eh? Tell the truth—yuh killed him then stole his coat.'

'No. I swear, a styke killed him.' I turned round to show him the hole in the coat.

The big troll rubbed his wart-covered chin. 'Stykes!' he said with a shudder. 'Better be careful, lads, if there's a clutch round the cave mouth. Becoming a spirit-cursed menace of late.'

'Maybe the guards or Ax sent him to spy on us—y'know, make sure we're working.'

'Doubt they'd send a dumb elf.'

One of them pulled the blanket off Moonshine, exposing her wings. 'What's this? Since when did winged horses pull mine carts? Maybe he's gonna fly the ore outta the mine, that

158

it?'

'Who are you? You checking up on us, sneak?' hissed the small troll.

'Yeah. What's in the bag?'

The trolls closed in, the big one snatching the bag from my shoulder. 'Got any grub, I'm starving.'

'Get off,' I protested but it was too late. The big troll shoved the bread into his mouth, and then threw the bag onto the ground.

'Hey, where's *our* bread? You should've known we'd all be hungry,' the troll taunted, prodding hard at my shoulder and forcing me to take several steps backwards till I fell against the mine cart. The next thing, the troll grabbed me, dumping me like a sack full of ore into the cart.

'Best not take any chances with this one.'

The trolls nodded to each other. 'How 'bout we give him a little ride?'

'Yeah, his last ride, then we'll put his horse to some proper work—some real mine work.'

'What are you doing?' I protested.

'Said you wanted to work in the

mine, didn't ya?'

They pushed the cart out of the alcove and into the gently sloping mine shaft till, picking up speed, it began trundling along on its own.

The trolls clapped each other on the back, laughing and waving goodbye. 'Enjoy the trip.'

'Run, Shy, and don't stop! Get out of here. Run!'

I clung to the side of the cart as the cave wall sped past and I wondered how I was going to get off. I was sure I'd break my leg if I jumped out. The cart was travelling quite fast and there was jagged rock everywhere.

I felt my foot scrape against something sharp and I winced with pain. I fumbled around at the bottom of the cart and picked up an axe. The trolls must have left it behind. It gave me an idea. Leaning over the side of the cart, I shoved the metal axe head between the wheel and the cart. Sparks spewed out, illuminating the dark mine shaft as, squealing like a low-belly pig, the cart began slowing down. Up ahead, the track curved and I jumped, rolling on the cave floor. The cart careered on into the blackness.

A saddlewood lamp flickered on the wall and I took it down. Three tunnels loomed and I stared desperately at them, images of stykes filling my mind. Losing the bag was gnawing at me too. No poison, no blowgun. But losing Moonshine was worse. What did I think I could do, even if Noose was down here?

*   *   *

Without really knowing why, I set off down the widest tunnel, keeping my eyes peeled on the cave roof, checking for moving stalactites. I prayed to the spirits that Moonshine hadn't been harmed and had made it to safety. I felt something furry scamper past my feet, at the same time hearing voices from deeper within the darkness. More miners maybe? I detected a tone of panic in the loudening voices. This, coupled with clanking noises as though buckets and tools were being cast down and the sudden parp of a horn, told me something was wrong.

Frantically I searched for a hiding place and saw one—a ledge and a hole, big enough for me to get inside, halfway up the mine wall. Climbing up the craggy rock, I crawled feet first into the hole, peering out into the mine.

Six or more trolls hurried through the mine towards the exit, one of them clutching a carved cattle horn.

I gasped as a white apparition of a snarling horned beast appeared, chasing them. It shimmered like Henk but was huge, almost filling the entire mine tunnel; its transparent glow was brighter, too, than the ghost's. Lashing out an enormous arm, the creature effortlessly tore a boulder from the mine wall and hurled it after the men, scattering them like bowling pins. The creature threw back its head in shrill laughter before excavating a bigger boulder, this time throwing it back into

162

the darkness. What kind of place was this? Man-eating stalactites and now some sort of demon spirit.

'Eat this, soul sucker!' said a gruff voice. A bigger troll dressed like the guard at the entrance emerged from deeper in the shaft, and discharged a huge weapon. A blinding beam of white light, like lightning, surged from the two glinting skull-shaped barrel ends. The bolt of energy tore into the rock above the apparition, causing a hail of rock pieces to rain down. The next shot went directly through the creature's chest. Its mouth opened in a deafening roar that shook the mineshaft as its ghostly body lit up. The roar became a shrill demonic scream, like the cries of a cavern full of rock bats. I couldn't bear it and covered my ears, my heart thundering like the Flyer at full steam. Then, before my eyes, the creature began to diminish; its ghostly outer form dropping off to reveal a phantom skeleton of pale, glowing bones—before they too began to fade, melting away to nothingness. And the creature was no more.

I lay silently for a while, listening to the groans and curses of the injured miners who'd been struck by the rock. Then suddenly I became aware of a different noise, like a faint wail coming from behind me, from somewhere inside the opening I was hiding in. The moan puzzled me, as it wasn't a gruff troll voice but the higher pitch of a young person. Exiting the vent, I turned to crawl back in, headfirst.

The wailing grew louder. 'Hello! Is anyone there?' I called.

'Y . . . yeah, in here. I'm trapped!'

I recognised the voice instantly. 'Jez! Jez, I'm coming, hang on!'

CHAPTER TEN

The Skull and the Treasure

I crawled further inside the passageway holding the lamp. Rubble was strewn all about making it difficult to pass.

'Will, in here. I'm stuck.'

Jez's voice came from behind a wall of rock debris.

'I'm here. How long you been in there?'

'Dunno, since the rock quake. All came down behind me, an' I couldn't get turned round to dig myself out.'

I gasped, recalling the quake yesterday that Henk said I'd been unconscious through after the dwarf baker hit me. She was mighty resilient; she'd been trapped for ages.

'Are you injured?'

'No, just a few scrapes an' bruises.'

'OK, hold on, I'll get you out of there.'

Clearing away the debris was hard work; my head throbbed as I strained to lift some of the bigger pieces of rock.

'Nearly there, Jez,' I called when I'd cleared enough to see her back.

A short while later I'd bust her out of her rock prison.

'I can't believe it,' she gasped. 'What are you doing here?'

'Crawled in to escape that demon thing tearing boulders outta the walls.'

'Mine wraith—quakes always shake them from the rock core. You were right to hide; wraith gets a hold of you it'll suck out your soul and leave you for the dust rats.'

I swallowed a lump in my throat. 'S'OK, a guard took it out with some kinda rifle . . .'

'Wynchester Demon Shot,' Jez finished. 'Elf invention—shoots some kinda magic fire dust, though not many know how. It's the only weapon that'll take out a wraith or a ghost.'

'Ghosts? But how can you take out something that's already dead?'

'Wraiths and ghosts might be dead but their spirits ain't and that's the part the demon shot wipes out.' Jez looked at me, 'Say, can you do magic?'

I remembered the conversation on board the flyer with the elf conductor then said, 'I gotta learn.'

I held up the lamp and suddenly realised that the narrow tunnel continued deep into the rock.

'Take it we're in an air vent then?'

'Yup.'

'I'd rather round up cattle than clear mine vents. I heard dust rats have teeth like daggers and grow as big as wood cats.'

Jez stroked the bone hilt of the knife in her belt. 'I've learned to look after myself. When I was trapped I was sure a big one would find me and get his revenge.'

'Didn't anyone bother to look for you?'

'Probably wouldn't even have missed me if I'd been squashed to death.'

I shuddered. 'And you're happy to work down here?'

'Ain't exactly got much choice. Pay's on time—well actually overdue since I been stuck here for a day—and I got nowhere else to go.' She rubbed her hands together. 'C'mon, I'll try and get you outta here. Troll guards don't take kindly to strangers pokin' around the mine.'

'Hang on, I've got a lead on that Noose, the bandit I'm looking for, he might be somehow connected with the tin mine. Only a couple of things have been bugging me: if Noose was hanging around down here then you'd have heard of him, right?'

'Reckon so, I've been crawling about in here for a long time.'

'And there's something else: why would a bank-robbing, cattle-rustling outlaw all of a sudden resign himself to life down a mineshaft? It doesn't make sense.' I paused. 'That is unless it isn't the tin mine he's working in at all.'

Jez frowned. 'I don't get ya.'

'*The deep mines?*' I breathed, my mind reeling. According to Jake, the deep mines had been closed up for over fifty years. Maybe that was it. Maybe all this had something to do with what Noose was pulling from the rock.

'It's not tin he's mining,' I said, my heart racing. 'It's . . . it's gold!'

169

'What?'

'The Klondex mine,' I gasped. 'The illegal mine that was closed down over fifty years ago. I can't believe I didn't think of it sooner.'

Jez was staring at me. 'What are you talking about?'

The seed of a plan was taking root in my head. 'These vents, do they run into the deep mines?'

'Ain't ever heard of the deep mines. But I have seen some older vents further up the ridge where I live.'

'Can you show me?' I removed the leather thong from around my neck, the saddlewood light reflecting off the beautiful pendant, a scorpion inside an oval of smooth amber. Yenene had given it to me when I was little. 'It's all I have left but it's yours if you'll help me.'

Jez's eyes widened, blinking like a marsh toad. She stared mesmerised by its ornate engraving. 'It's beautiful but I can't take it. You just saved my life, should be me giving *you* something.'

'And you saved mine, hauling me onto the roof of the Flyer to escape that whip-tail.'

She took it and put it back over my head. 'Keep it. And of course I'll help you.' She dusted herself down and slowly crawled on her hands and knees along the vent. 'C'mon.'

I followed, asking, 'Are you OK to crawl?'

'I'm fine,' she replied. 'Just glad to get outta there!'

I thought of my bag. I was sure the troll miners had ransacked its contents by now and much as it bothered me, I knew I'd no choice but to leave it. Finding it would be hard enough, finding it with the darts and poison intact was more than I could hope for. I'd just have to figure out another way to bring in Noose.

We crawled for what felt like ages. My knees ached and my hands were scratched and sore. Then Jez suddenly announced, 'Wanna see something creepy?'

What could be creepier than stykes and mine wraiths? I thought. 'Sure.'

'Used to give me skin pimples the size of warts, but now I use it as a vent landmark . . . here it is.'

At first I couldn't see anything other than a few clumps of old rock but as I looked closer I could just make out two dark orbits, then teeth, both surrounded by dusty white bone . . . a skull!

'Debris from rock quakes has almost buried him over time.'

'Do you know who it is?' I asked.

'Nope.'

'Wonder what happened to him?'

'Leg bone's trapped under a huge

172

boulder, maybe he got stuck like me.'

'How long's he been here?'

'Hard to say. Poor critter. Dust rats would've stripped him in hours.'

'Kind of a gruesome end.'

'You ain't kidding.'

'But what was he doing? They don't look like troll bones.'

'Maybe hiding from somebody.'

I shivered as I crawled over the skeleton to follow Jez, then squinted as a pang of bright light hit me square in the eyes.

'Where are we going?'

'Shortcut to a vent I think might lead to the deep mines you're talking about. We have to go out onto the ridge.'

A couple of days in Deadrock had taken its toll on my eyes. I'd grown so used to the dim glow of saddlewood that I'd almost forgotten about what blazed at the end of the vent . . . daylight.

*   *   *

I watched Jez disappear out the hole before I too emerged, blinking, onto

173

the western arm of the megalith. I sucked in a big lungful of the fresh air whipped up from the Wastelands that loomed far below. I looked down, but only for a second as it made my head swim, and realised it was the same place I'd visited yesterday: one of the many ledges near Pike's Ridge.

Jez was panting. 'It's a short climb from here but I gotta stop for a while. I need a drink before I pass out.'

She crawled along the narrow ledge and sat down, her legs dangling over the edge. Moving a stone from a small hole that had been hollowed out of the rock, she reached inside, taking out an earthen jug. She took a long gulp before handing it to me. I drank my fill, spat out a bug then followed her gaze toward a distant cluster of tornadoes.

'Say, why you wearing a guard's coat?'

'I'm undercover.'

I shuffled along the ledge but lost my balance. Jez shot an arm out to steady me. Rock and dust plummeted down below. 'Thanks.'

'S'OK,' said Jez, blushing. 'You'd

most likely've splattered all over the railroad,' she went on, matter-of-factly.

I glanced down, realising that below us on a wider ledge lay the rail track, that ran all the way up to Oretown. I thought of my grandma and the other ranchers and suddenly felt very homesick. I was sure I could smell the faintest whiff of sixberry pie blowing on the wind.

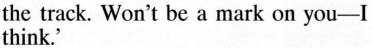

'Maybe you should forget about Noose and start walking,' Jez remarked. 'If the Flyer comes you just lie down in the middle of the track. Won't be a mark on you—I think.'

I wiped my mouth with my sleeve. 'I'm not going home without Noose or Moonshine.'

Jez rummaged in the hole again, stirring my curiosity. 'Say, what else you got in there?'

She winked. 'Call this my treasure chest. I'll show you something.'

She took out a semicircular brass-coloured object about the length of her forearm, angular and etched with fine notches in a sort of scale. It was the kind of object that even if you didn't know what it was, still looked very intriguing, almost magical. I, however, knew exactly what it was.

I muttered, 'Eldon,' and fished in my pocket, under the troll's coat, for the newspaper cutting. Feeling my breath quicken, I flattened the crumpled paper in my dirty palm and stared in disbelief. 'Where'd you get this,' I asked, half blotting out the answer I hoped wouldn't come back at me.

QUAKE BREAKTHROUGH!

Story by Digger Scoops

Inventor, Eldon Overland, proudly displays his latest invention for measuring rock quakes. Overland has devoted years to studying rock quakes and hopes that his investigations will one day help make things a bit less shaky for Oretown folk. Pictured with him is his good friend Deputy Sheriff, Dan Gallows, who has promised Eldon the full support of the sheriff's department during his research.

Gallows and Overland

Jez motioned a hand toward the vent. 'Right by the skeleton. Beautiful, ain't it?'

I stared back at the vent, a sick feeling rising in my throat.

'You all right? You gone as pale as

176

a mine wraith,' said Jez, glancing over my shoulder at the cutting. 'Wait a minute, that thing that elf's holding looks just like . . .' She held the brass-coloured object up beside the picture. 'I don't believe it . . . you knew him, didn't you?'

I nodded slowly. 'His name was Eldon Overland. A friend of my pa's, a scientist. He was doing studies on the rock down there on Pike's Ridge. He went missing last year, around the same time my pa died. In fact my pa was on his way to meet him when Noose attacked.'

'I'm sorry.'

So now I could tell Grandma that Eldon hadn't been blown over the ridge by a tornado. Seemed he'd been working, taking measurements of the area when he must've discovered the vent. Maybe the readings from his equipment had led him there. Had there been a quake? Had a boulder trapped his leg, leaving him at the mercy of hungry dust rats? I'd probably never know for sure but it looked like Eldon's passion for studying rock

177

quakes had cost him his life.

'Can we go?' I asked solemnly.

Jez nodded, and she climbed up the steep rock face like her hands were made of glue. I struggled to keep up. Where the rock levelled into another small ledge, Jez moved some tangleweed, exposing a smaller vent.

'Reckon this could be the vent to the deep mines.'

I rubbed my knees. They were bleeding and sore. 'How long is it?'

'Never crawled it—ain't one of my vents. And I don't intend to either unless Ax pays me. Which reminds me, I gotta go see him. You OK if I catch up with you later?'

I nodded. 'Probably best if I go alone. Oh, but before you go, can I borrow your blade?' Taking Jez's knife, I cut the sleeves off the guard's coat and bound my knees. Then, cutting some material off the bottom of my shirt, I did the same to my grazed hands.

I handed her back the knife. 'Thanks.'

'Goodbye, Will.'

She turned to make her way back across the ledge when I called, 'Wait.' Before she could stop me, I quickly slipped off the pendant and put it round her neck.

'No. Told ya . . .'

'I want you to have it, Jez, for your treasure chest.'

'Treasure chest, no way. If I keep it I'll wear it, I'll wear it all the time.'

'Then keep it.'

She smiled. 'Ain't gonna argue. Thanks. Goodbye. And good luck.'

*   *   *

As I crawled, the narrow walls seemed to close around me as though the vent was trying to squeeze me to death before I even got to the deep mines. After a while time seemed to melt away, replaced by the shuffle of my knees on the rock. I'd long since given up trying to work out how Jez managed to spend all day every day crawling through the vents and still keep her sanity. Fears began to creep up alongside me. What if there was a quake and I got stuck like Jez? Was this even the right way? Had Moonshine got out of the mine alive? *Shuffle! Shuffle!* So fixed was my gaze on the floor of the vent that it was some time before I realised it was getting wider. At one point I was grateful to be able to move into a sitting position and rest for a while, stretching out my aching legs. Rubble was strewn all around and I figured the cavern might have been formed during a rock quake.

I had to force myself to start out again as I could see the vent begin to narrow not far ahead. *Shuffle! Shuffle!* I hadn't travelled far when my hand touched something that didn't fit, something soft. It reminded me of the straw Moonshine ate back at the ranch only it was coarser and scattered all over the vent. I raised the torch and saw that up ahead, it became so dense that it plugged up the entire passageway. I clawed at some with my fingers, trying to dig a way through, when I heard rustling noises beyond the blockage. Something was there.

The next thing, white teeth flashed in the lamplight, lunging at me from the foliage. A huge dust rat! Instinctively I flung up my arm, the assailant sinking its incisors through the material of my coat into flesh. I let out a yell that echoed far back through the vent, probably to the western arm itself. The dirty brown animal wasn't letting go and, beady eyes fixed on my throat, it was no doubt cursing its miscalculation.

Rocking back to rest on my heels, I flung my free hand behind me. I was sure I'd just grazed my knee on some broken pieces of boulder. Like a coach spider gone crazy, my fingers fumbled around until . . . yes! I brought the hand-sized lump of rock down onto the rat's head with all the force I could muster. The noise of the splintering bone almost made me retch as the animal, spattering my coat with its blood, fell to the ground.

Heart racing, I slowly clawed my way through the rest of the straw, rock at the ready. But there were no more dust rats; the others had obviously fled into the network of vents. At least now I knew how Jez made a living, for what it was worth, though I sure could have done with that little bone-handled knife she carried with her.

In time the *shuffle shuffle* was joined by different noises coming from further along the passageway. Grinding, digging noises, coupled with a rhythmic, deeper thudding. Even in bound hands I felt the rock below me tremble. But what was causing it?

Finally I reached the end of the vent.

'The deep mines,' I breathed.

*　　　*　　　*

I looked inside, scarcely able to take in what I saw. Troll miners worked busily, swinging axe heads into several rock faces in an enormous, dimly-lit chamber. They shovelled chunks of rock into carts which, once full, they wheeled over to a circular pit in the middle of the chamber, tipping the rocks into the pit. Completing the process, a muscular ogre slowly pushed a large stone ball around the pit, grinding the rocks. Two scowling guards stood near what appeared to be an exit tunnel. And there in the midst of it all, puffing on a bacca-weed pipe, barking orders, stood Noose.

He wore a dusty bark-cloth shirt, soaking with sweat and unbuttoned at the top to reveal a ripple of scales. And just like the barman in the saloon, I saw something wriggle under his shirt. He had dark eyes and wore the same scowl from the wanted poster, only his hair was longer and dirtier and his bloated nose and protruding chin had sprouted a lot more warts. He licked his lips with a horrible green tongue.

For a place that should have been closed up, it sure was a hive of industry. How could this go on without anyone knowing? Jake had said that mining the deep mines would weaken and eventually spell the destruction of the western arm.

I suddenly realised that Noose was not giving orders but yelling at someone who appeared to be tied to the millstone, though I couldn't see clearly because a group of miners had

gathered round to watch, obscuring my view. Ax was near Noose, I recognised him from yesterday when he'd ignored the exhausted miners' pleas to still his whip.

'For the last time, where's the boy?' Noose was drawling loudly.

'I told you, I don't know!' came the reply.

'Yer lyin'. Ya said ya was trapped in the vent an' that someone helped ya!'

'Yeah, but I didn't see who helped me, they were gone by the time I could move again. My leg got hurt pretty bad.'

To my horror, I caught the briefest glimpse of the subject of Noose's wrath. JEZ! I gasped in revulsion. How could this be? It seemed like I'd only just left her.

'Shut yer mouth.' Noose ripped the pendant from round her neck. 'Since when does a dwarf wear an elf pendant?'

Ax added, 'And all this near to where Hegg an' the others say they saw the intruder . . . an elf boy!'

'Ya tell 'im 'bout the deep mines?'

'How could I tell him about a place I didn't even know existed?'

'Yer lyin'.' He struck her in the face.

I noticed something stir beneath his partly unbuttoned shirt and the heads of two black snakes oozed from his stomach region, tongues flickering, uncoiling to hiss loudly in her face.

'It's the truth!'

'Ya helped him?'

'He helped me!' she blurted out. 'I was trapped. No one else was rushing to see if I was OK after the quake. But then I don't know where he went, probably climbed out at the western arm.'

'Somethin' stinks 'bout this. Kid's been askin' questions about me in town then he shows up and starts pokin' 'bout my mine. Well, I'm gonna find 'im then am gonna crush his liddle head under this stone.' He waved an arm toward a group of miners, shouting, 'Down yer tools and search the mine. Search everywhere, d'ya hear. Bring him t' me alive!'

'Whadda we do with the dwarf?' murmured Ax.

'Kill her. She's seen too much.' He spat on the ground in derision. *'Urgala!'* The ogre stood up, pushing the millstone lever, causing the heavy boulder to begin rolling forward.

'So long, dwarf.'

I knew I had only one option. Without a second thought, I crawled out of the vent.

CHAPTER ELEVEN

THE SNAKE-BELLIED TROLL

I scrabbled from my hide-out into the mine chamber, climbing down the wall. 'Let her go!'

Noose held up an arm and the ogre froze. It fell quiet. Dark troll eyes burned into my flesh. More snakes poured from Noose's shirt as he strode towards me, scowling.

'Well now, looky what crawled out of a hole in the rock. If it ain't the liddle dust rat, finally decided to show his face.'

The belly-snakes, with their oily black skin and thin heads, fixed their black beady eyes on me while Noose, his breath rancid, grabbed me by the coat.

'Been causin' me some trouble, kid. Who sent ya?'

'No one sent me.' I decided there was no point in telling him anything but the truth. 'I'm a bounty seeker and I've

. . . I've come to bring you in,' I blurted out, my voice quivering more than I'd have liked.

The mine chamber erupted in laughter.

Examining the coat I wore, Noose growled, 'My guard's dead, elf boy. Ya killed my guard!'

'No, a styke killed him, I swear.'

'Were no styke in 'im, accordin' to my men.'

'I took it out to get the coat.'

'Lie to me an' I'll kill ya now with my bare hands.'

'It's the truth.'

'Reckon yer spyin' for the High Sheriff.'

'Told you, I'm a bounty seeker.'

'Most bounty slayers got themselves a horse. Where's yer horse?'

'She bolted when the troll miners found me.'

Noose seemed to ponder this, rubbing his warty chin. 'Yer pretty stupid but ya got guts, I'll say that for ya. Just a pity I'm gonna spill 'em all over this here millstone, yours an' your liddle girlfriend's both. Then, when the dust rats have finished with ya, maybe we'll hang you up beside ol' Zeb Klondex here.' He paced to where a rope dangled. I looked up and gasped. The rope was attached to a skeleton suspended from the mine roof and as Noose pulled the rope, it began to rattle, bones juddering and jaw opening and closing in a sort of macabre dance. Noose laughed hard, coughing and hacking up a mouthful of phlegm, which he spat onto my boot.

I felt a knot of icy fear in my chest. A desperate powerlessness gripped me—the speed at which my plan was crumbling filled me with cold fear.

'Y . . . you can't kill me,' I stammered, feeling my throat tighten unbearably. 'There are others, they'll come looking for me.'

With a gloved hand, Noose lifted me off the ground, pulling me closer. The belly-snakes hissed and spat at me, and I could feel his hot, stinking breath on my face.

'Never tell me what I can't do,' he growled through clenched teeth. 'Tie him up beside the girl while I gets me something to drink.'

'Two of us could push the stone, boss.'

'Yeah, why should the ogre get all the fun?' the miners grumbled.

Noose strode off. 'Sure, why not. You can cast lots to see who gets to squish 'em.' Then he glanced back at me, grinning. 'My men don't get much in the way of entertainment.'

My heart pounded as the ogre lifted me, draping me face-up beside Jez on top of the huge millstone. I struggled but it was pointless, like a gutfish writhing in the hands of a giant. Rope was flung across my chest and legs then pulled taut.

I turned to Jez. 'Sorry you had to get caught up in all this.'

'S'OK, ain't your fault,' she replied, 'an' it's still a quicker death than being eaten by dust rats back where I was trapped.'

To my horror I watched the troll miners eagerly gathering bits of old rope to use for the lot casting.

'Don't give up, Jez. We'll get out of here, I'll think of something.'

When Noose returned carrying a bottle of Boggart's Breath I cried, 'This whole thing is illegal. You're ripping the stability from the western arm, causing rock quakes. Thousands of folk could die if Oretown collapses into the Wastelands.'

'Yer knowledge of geology and the mine here's pretty impressive, but as far as I'm concerned, Oretown falling into the Wastelands wouldn't be much of a loss to the West Rock.'

'You're scum, Noose Wormworx.'

'An' you're dead . . .' He paused. 'Heck, pardon my manners but I figure it's only right findin' out whose guts I'm gonna be squashin'. What's yer name, elf boy?'

'Gallows, Will Gallows. My pa was deputy of Oretown till you gunned him down during a shoot-out at Pike's Ridge.'

'Well now—this is interestin'.' He drummed a warty finger on his chin. 'Pike's Ridge, now you're takin' me back. Oh yeah, I remember, though

I wouldn't call it a shoot-out. Yer ol' man weren't much of a shot. It was over in seconds. Somethin' kinda poetic 'bout a Noose finishing off a Gallows, don't ya think?'

Furious, I wrestled with my bonds. 'In a fair gunfight my pa would've put more holes in you than a pepperpot. Place like this suits you, hiding under a rock like the clattersnake you are.'

'Hiding? Oh no, Noose don't hide from nobody. I'd call it protectin' my investment. If you dug up a treasure chest ya wouldn't walk away and leave it, now would ya?'

A shout from the mine floor and I realised that the troll miners were in a final head-to-head for the right to squash our guts under the millstone.

'Time you both were dead. Honourable gesture, though, ya comin' all this way to avenge yer pa's killer. But see, most bounty slayers come after me with a posse.' He craned his neck looking over the millstone then burst into a fit of laughter. 'You talk about folks comin' looking for ya but the reality is—ya ain't got a soul with

ya!'

As he spoke, a dirty pale horse with a ghostly mount galloped into the mine followed by a figure on foot, brandishing a revolver in his shimmering hand. It was Henk riding an almost unrecognisable Moonshine! And the ghost on foot was Jake, who expertly shot through the ropes that lashed us both to the millstone, freeing us to sit up. I noticed that Jake had my bag with the darts and poison in it, slung over his shoulder. The troll miners must've dumped it somewhere and Jake found it.

Henk grinned. 'Shy told us you could do with some spiritual help.'

Jake blew on the barrel of his gun then twirled it around his finger. 'I came along to keep a grip on things.' Then, an apologetic tone to his voice, he added, 'By the way, kid, that poker game, you won it fair and square.' He unleashed a barrage of gunfire into the air, scattering the terrified miners and Noose who ran for cover. Ax fell to the ground clutching his chest.

When the gunfire ceased, Noose

cried, 'Well, well, seems the sky cavalry's arrived!' then he turned to address the dust ogre. *'Um Urghala!'*

Reacting to Noose's instruction in its own tongue, the ogre suddenly roared and, grabbing the lever, began pushing the millstone forward. We fell into the pit, right into the path of the boulder.

Jake saw what was happening and put three rounds in the ogre's belly. But apart from making it even angrier, they did little else, bouncing off his impenetrable rough ogre hide. Moonshine galloped to sink her incisors into the ogre's fleshy heel but it kicked her off. I grabbed Jez's arm and pulled her clear of the stone, then I ran to take cover near Henk. But Jez shot off in the other direction towards the vent.

Signalling a cease-fire, Henk cried, 'Let the boy come with us and no one gets hurt.'

'Been responsible for a whole lot o' phantoms in my time,' Noose replied from the cover of a barrel stack, 'but it'll be a sorry day I start takin' orders from one.' And reaching behind his shoulder he drew a Wynchester Demon Shot from a holster strapped across his back. I immediately recognised it as the same weapon the troll guard had used on the mine wraith and yelled, 'Take cover!'

'What the blazes is that?'

'Keep away from it,' I called. 'It can snuff out ghosts.'

The bolt of lightning-bright energy seared through the air as Henk dived behind a crevice, narrowly avoiding the lethal projectile.

Most of the miners were unarmed and, terrified by the flighty ghost unleashing a storm of bullets, they ran, stumbling for the exit tunnel, some of them helped along by a hefty kick from Moonshine. Those who remained had only revolvers, which were totally useless against the already-dead ghosts. Only Noose's weapon had the power to quench a spirit.

The ogre tore off the leather harness, separating itself from the ore-grinding pit. Then with its massive arms it grabbed a boulder and pointlessly hurled it at Jake, doing no more damage than smashing a mine cart to smithereens.

'Give it up, ya figmentations!' Noose shouted. Then in the ogre's tongue, he cried, *'Umgo urula ruh!'*

The ogre, like a loyal dog, crashed over to stand in front of Noose taking a hail of bullets from Jake, who seemed determined to finish off the lumbering beast. But the bullets just bounced off the ogre's impenetrable skin.

Jake's fury, however, also made him careless and with his cover in smithereens, thanks to the boulder, he gave Noose room to get a shot on target. The room bloomed in light as Jake crumpled over, the gun flying from his hand. Smoke spewed from his mouth as his body—twitching and fizzling in the gloomy cavern—began vaporising.

Noose seemed to sense a quick victory and moved forward, seeing Henk unarmed. He fired at the ghost but instead caught me in the forehead, sending me flying backwards across the cavern. The pain was excruciating but passed quickly leaving me only with a few bruises from my fall. The weapon was useless on the living and Noose cursed his bad aim, unholstering his revolver.

Suddenly a shot rang out and Noose staggered backwards, clutching his leg.

'Wha . . .?' I turned to see Henk shakily clutching Jake's gun, a stunned look on his face. 'Henk, your grip—it's back!' I cried.

'Mortifications! I . . . I don't believe it,' Henk gasped. 'Truly never thought the touch of cold steel could feel so good. You OK?'

Noose was shouting as he retreated for the cover of the barrel stack. 'Ya can't win, phantom. Throw down your weapon or I'll snuff out your soul for good!'

Henk shouted, 'We've got to take the ogre out, it's protecting him!'

I noticed the bag lying on the ground where Jake had been snuffed out. Moonshine was standing near it and I called to her. 'Shy,

toss me the bag.'

Moonshine grabbed the bag with her teeth and flung it across the mine floor but it landed just short of its target. Furious at her involvement, Noose fired at her and she bolted for the cover of the mine entrance.

Grabbing a stick, I stretched it out towards the bag. Noose let out a barrage of gunfire. After a bit of fishing, I managed to hook the bag strap onto the end of the stick and drag it towards me. I opened it. Miraculously the jar was still intact but the little beaded pouch was missing, probably stolen. I pulled out the blowgun, now broken in several places and clutched the longest piece.

'I've been busting a gut to find out what was so important 'bout that bag and all the time it weren't nothing but a jarful of jam,' said Henk.

'Poison,' I corrected, noticing something else in the bottom of the bag. I grasped the single dart. 'OK, I think I've got an idea how to take the ogre out.' I plastered the dart with poison so thickly that it oozed from the tip, then placed it inside the blowgun.

'Can see cartwheels turning in your head, Will. What you thinking?'

'That I need to get closer. The poison will take him out quickly, though this pipe's too short for a long-range shot; plus I only got one dart so it has to count.' I gazed across the mine. 'That upturned cart over there. If I could get to it I'd have a clear shot.'

'I'll cover you.'

'No way, it's too dangerous. The demon shot'll destroy you. I can make it.'

'I'll cover you,' Henk smiled. 'Remember what I said 'bout still having something to do to earn my way up above? Well dang it if I ain't sure this is it.' He extended a ghostly hand. 'Partners?'

I reached out and shook, feeling Henk's cold grip for the first time. 'Partners,' I echoed, smiling.

'Now, go for it!'

I went for it, darting across the

cavern, zigzagging. I heard Henk fire repeatedly at Noose and the ogre, but Noose—the ogre for his cover—managed to return fire at me, and a hail of bullets sparked off the mine cart just as I dived behind it. The ogre opened its mouth wide in a roar of protest at my manoeuvre. That was my cue—I put the blowgun to my lips, aimed, then blew sharply. The dart tore through the mouldy mine air and embedded in the ogre's black lolling tongue. Gagging and snorting, the ogre clasped its jaw shut, chewing up the dart before spitting it out. 'Pteeewaghh!'

Enraged, the ogre scooped up a boulder, tossing it at me. But it crashed short of its target; perhaps the poison was taking effect, I thought. I had worried that it wouldn't work against a creature of the ogre's size and bulk. When the ogre lifted another larger boulder, I figured I should make a move. I signalled to Henk that I was coming back. Henk read the signal and leaned out, raining one shot after another towards the ogre. But the revolver only had so many bullets and soon the hammer clicked against the empty chamber. As the ogre began to wobble, I turned to see Noose, now crouching beside the barrel stack, aim the blaster . . .

'Get back, Henk!' I cried.

But my warning was too late and Noose unleashed a fiercesome bolt of energy directly at Henk. He caught the full impact in the head, which flew off his shoulders, vaporising as it streaked across the cave. The rest of him vaporised along with it.

'Noooooooooooooo!'

I watched in horror as the pale mist that had once been Henk, gradually faded away.

'Henk, where are you?' I cried. 'Come back, you can't go.'

A rush of tears filled my eyes, blurring the gloomy cavern into a haze of purple light. I felt like I was going to throw up. Henk was gone. I'd only known him for a few days, but in that time we'd become partners and good friends. Now he'd vaporised, like a puff of bacca-weed smoke. I couldn't take it all in, it was almost too much to bear; but then Henk's last words came to me out of nowhere, *Remember what I said 'bout still having something to do to earn my way up above? Well dang it if I ain't sure this is it.*

I swallowed hard. I suddenly had a strange sense that Henk was all right, that he was in a better place, no longer an outlaw of the spirit world, like he'd said. There was comfort, too, in that maybe I'd helped him get there.

I blinked away the tears and Noose came into focus. He stood, stone still, in front of the ogre on the other side of the cavern. A cluster of hissing black snakes reared up from his stomach, tongues flickering.

'Just you and me now, kid,' he snarled. 'Why don't you give it up?'

'Never!' I called back, still crouched behind the boulder that had been my cover for most of the gun battle. I caught sight of Moonshine lurking in the shadows of the exit tunnel and signalled to her to stay put. 'I won't give up till you're behind bars.'

Noose roared with laughter. 'In case

you hadn't noticed, your pathetic little ghost posse are no longer with us.' He threw down the Wynchester Demon Shot. He didn't need it anymore. From here on, it was the living against the low-life.

The ogre let out a deafening roar and my heart pounded like it was trying to jail-break its way out of my ribcage. The frog poison hadn't worked. Maybe the dart had failed to penetrate its great slug of a tongue properly, or maybe it was just too big and ugly. The beast lumbered forward, bearing dagger-sharp teeth, but Noose outstretched an arm as if to tell it that this was *his* battle, and it halted.

'Why don't we sort this out in the open?' Noose cried, unfastening one of the many gun belts strapped round his waist. He flung it across the cavern where it landed on the ground in front of the boulder. 'You were shootin' yer mouth off earlier about a fair gunfight so let's go. What could be fairer than just you an' me facin' each other in a quick-draw gunfight?'

I stared at the weapon; the black

gun metal glinted in the saddlewood light, the holster was black too, and decorated with a jewelled skull.

'I'm no gunslinger, I . . . I don't wanna shoot you,' I stuttered.

'Scared, huh?' he goaded. 'I take back what I said 'bout ya havin' guts. Guess yer afraid in case yer a lousy shot like yer pa.'

Fuming, I emerged from behind the rock and lifted the gun, taking far too long with my shaking hands to fasten it around my waist. Noose was wrong. Pa was a crack shot with a six-shooter but said that killing was a cowardly way out of a situation and that it never solved anything. He'd never killed a man in his life. And even though I was fastening a gun belt to my waist, I knew I didn't want to shoot Noose. What I really wanted was some inspiration. What was I going to do next?

Then came a glimmer of hope.

When I looked up from fastening the gun belt, I was sure I saw the ogre wobble slightly. Was the frog poison beginning to take effect? If it was, there might just be a chance I could use the distraction to do something; maybe if Noose turned round I could shoot him in the leg, get his gun, and then poison him with the last of the frog poison.

Noose grinned. 'Well now, that's more like it. Just whenever ya feel yer ready to die, kid.'

He pinned back one side of his coat with his arm, revealing his holster and gun and laid his right hand beside it, in the quick-draw position. I noticed his trigger finger twitch a few times.

The ogre began to wail, its eyes rolling in their sockets, clutching its head with its hands. Now I was certain the frog poison was working.

'Shaddup, ya big galumph!' Noose shouted, annoyed by the ogre's disturbance but not enough to take his eyes off me so I could try to shoot him in the leg. 'Yer wreckin' my concentration. Come on, kid, go for yer gun. Ya know ya wanna shoot ol' Noose; ya know ya wanna kill me and avenge yer pa. Why, it's running through you like poison.'

It was. But the frog poison was

running through the ogre a lot faster, and that creature was looking more and more unsteady on its feet.

'Gettin' kinda tired waitin',' Noose drawled. 'I've got me a bottle here.' Slowly he put his left hand in his pocket, removing the bottle of Boggart's Breath he'd been drinking earlier. 'So here's the deal: I'm gonna toss up this here bottle, then when it falls we draw, OK?'

Still I said nothing. I stood frozen to the spot, mind and body numb with fear, staring past him at the ogre that staggered like a drunk in the Deadrock saloon.

'Don't matter whether you agree or not,' Noose went on, 'I'm tossin' it anyways—here goes.'

And he launched the bottle high up into the cavern, almost scraping the mine roof, until it plummeted back towards the ground. I held my breath, my eyes darting between the bottle and the ogre—that had now lost consciousness and was falling forward . . . forward towards Noose.

The bottle hit the ground, shattering

 on the rocky mine floor. L i g h t n i n g quick, Noose's twitching hand was round the butt of his gun and he had the weapon fully out of the holster. But before he could pull the trigger, the ogre crashed on top of him, squeezing the life breath from his body.

And the mine fell silent. I watched Noose's foot, poking out from under the ogre, twitch until it was still. Then I stood silently, listening to the ogre's laboured breathing turn to a deep snoring.

Moonshine trotted out of her hiding place in the tunnel.

'S'over, Shy.'

'Thank the spirits. You OK?'

'I'm fine. You?'

She snorted. 'Yeah, I'm OK. But Jake and Henk.'

'Might not be so bad,' I said. 'As Henk once said, they were outlaws of the spirit world, caught down here for some reason.'

Moonshine glanced upwards. 'You

mean there's a chance they've gone up to the Great Spirit world?'

I nodded. 'S'only good folks up there and they don't come much better than Jake and Henk.' I stroked her nose. 'You done good too, Shy, fetching help. I couldn't have done any of this without you. Your pa would've been proud of you.'

Moonshine whinnied. 'Yours too. And I'd do it again, we're a team, remember.'

At the millstone I recovered the amber pendant that Noose had ripped off Jez's neck earlier. 'Where's Jez?'

'Must've escaped back up the vent.'

Moving to the spot where Henk had been cut down, I lifted the gun and stood for a while, not knowing why but just because it felt right. I ran my fingers over the bone handle. Henk hadn't had too long to enjoy his new ghost grip.

Then, hefting the bag over my shoulder, I led Moonshine sombrely out of the mine.

CHAPTER TWELVE

Betrayal

I staggered, exhausted, into the exit tunnel. Moonshine ambled along beside me; head drooped and this time she wasn't acting. Neither of us spoke. Saddlewood lamps were few and far between and most of the tunnel was dark and gloomy, which fitted my mood. I felt my way through the darker areas, stumbling rather than walking on the uneven ground, thinking about the shoot-out, about Jez, about everything.

The click of a trigger jolted me from my thoughts.

'Who's there?'

I froze, struggling to identify the voice calling from the gloom. It was oddly recognisable, it was just that it didn't fit down here, didn't fit at all. Raising the gun, I peered into the gloom. The purple glow of a distant branch lit a portly figure moving towards me. A tin star glinted on its chest.

'Boy? That you, boy?' the figure wheezed.

'S . . . Sheriff Slugmarsh? What are you doing here?'

'Spirits alive, tell me I'm seeing things.'

'I . . . I found Noose,' I blurted out. 'He's dead, buried under a dust ogre and he hasn't been hiding. Tin mine's nothing but a front. He reopened the old Klondex gold mine—the rock quakes, he was to blame for all of it. The western arm could crumble any day . . .'

'Woah, hold your horses, boy. You say Noose is dead?'

'I darted a dust ogre and it fell on top of him.'

'Hand me that gun, everything's gonna be all right.'

'C'mon you gotta see this.' I handed the weapon over then took the sheriff into the mine.

'You blow me away, boy,' the sheriff cried, gazing round at the carnage then at Noose's foot protruding from underneath the snoring ogre. 'Seems I

212

got you all wrong—you ain't so crazy after all.'

In the dim purple light I could see his face redden. He was sweating profusely and removed his hat to sweep a few sticky strands of hair over his bald head.

'Don't make sense though,' I frowned. 'With the deep mines being regularly inspected by the sky cavalry, how could this have been allowed to go on for so long?'

'Cos they ain't been doing their job—but you have. Seems you got more than a little of your old man in ya.' A tinge of venom in the sheriff's voice made me uneasy. His gold tooth glinted in the half-light as with a fraught chuckle he added, 'Just a pity you won't be collecting the reward money.'

I felt an icy chill run up and down my spine. 'Won't be? What do you mean? Poster says dead or alive, though I never wanted him dead.'

'*Never wanted him dead.*' The sheriff's voice tone was mocking. 'Self-righteous little half-breed. Well he *is* dead. You killed him. And it's gonna take an age to sort out this mess!'

Moonshine pawed the ground, whinnying nervously. My head swam. The sheriff wasn't making any sense. 'Mess? I don't understand. You . . . you're angry . . .'

'A n g r y !' S l u g m a r s h fumed. 'Oh, I'm way past angry, boy. I was *angry* when you woke me up slapping Noose's face on my desk. I was *angry* when you made me look a fool in front of that whip-tail. But this, killing a friend o' mine while at the same time hacking a great big pickaxe through the Slugmarsh retirement fund. Oh no, I'm way past angry, boy—I . . . I'm SEETHING!' And trembling with

214

rage, he pointed the gun at me.

Moonshine reared up, her forelegs kicking the air, but I seized her reins. 'No, Shy, leave it.'

Slugmarsh swung the gun at her but held his fire when, still baring her teeth, she allowed me to restrain her.

'Y . . . you and Noose,' I stammered. 'You knew about everything?'

'Are you really dumb enough to think he could've got away with all this without someone knowing 'bout it? Ain't Mid-Rock that inspects the deep mines. That task was entrusted to Oretown's sheriff's office years ago.'

'Noose reopened the mine and you turned a blind eye?'

'Now you're getting the picture.'

'Then Eldon . . . Eldon knew! He told Pa, didn't he?'

'Crazy ol' elf told your pa all right,' Slugmarsh sneered. 'Told him he'd figured out what was causing all the rock quakes. That he'd even heard noises coming from somewhere in the

215

vicinity of the old gold mine.'

Slugmarsh took out a small bottle of Boggart's Breath from his pocket. Removing the lid, he took a long swig. 'Course your pa then relays all this information to me, starts pokin' his nose in where it don't belong, askin' if I kept records of inspections of the old mine site, saying maybe we should check it out. I told him I'd checked it out recently but he kept at me, just wouldn't let it go.' He paused for another swig.

I stared at him. 'So?'

'To get him off my back I agreed and we rode down together, stopping along the way to see the elf. What your pa didn't know was that I'd told Noose to meet us halfway, make it look like a botched raid on the Flyer. But there was so much smoke from the Flyer your pa got a good shot at Noose; caught him plumb on the shoulder— could've killed him if it weren't for . . .'

'For what?' I swallowed. 'If it weren't for what?'

'Well with Noose injured, I had to step in and sort things out. As you've already witnessed, you can't rely on Noose for anything, what with him being a dumb troll. I just let him fly around making a big noise to all those witness onlookers in the first class carriage of the Flyer while I . . . I put a bullet in your pa—shutting that big mouth o' his for good!'

I gasped. 'You murdered my pa? Your own deputy?'

'Had no option, boy.' He aimed the gun at my head. Moonshine let out a loud whinny. 'Just like I got no option right now either . . .'

I looked him in the eye and saw his face contort into an uglier than usual grimace. The gun dropped from his hand and he fell limply onto the ground; a familiar bone-handled knife protruded from his shoulder blade. I stood rooted to the ground as Jez's pale eyes blinked in the dimness of the vent. 'Well don't just stand there,' she cried, 'help me down.'

'Jez, where'd you get to?'

'I was crawling along the vent when I figured I couldn't just leave you. So I turned back. Who is this?'

Sweat dripped from my forehead. 'The Sheriff of Oretown, believe it or not. It was him who killed my pa, not Noose.'

I helped her climb down and she poked him with her foot. 'Ain't dead, he's still breathin'.'

The sound of voices drifted from the mine tunnel and Jez added, 'You should get out of here; the troll miners won't be spooked for ever, they'll be back.'

'Yeah, I'm going.' I took out the pendant, tied the broken thong then I handed it to Jez.

'Great, you found it.'

'Noose must've dropped it near the millstone.'

'I'd have hated to have lost it.'

'I'll give you a ride to the outside, if you like?' I said, taking Moonshine's rein.

Jez nodded, pulling the pendant over her head.

We rode quickly but carefully, not stopping, through the maze of dimly lit tunnels, out of the deep mines, then on along the main shaft of the tin mine.

We bumped into a few troll miners but luckily no one tried to stop us. My heart leaped when we cantered out of the mine entrance, heading past the freight station towards the Deadrock tunnel.

'What now?' Jez asked.

'Mid-Rock City to see the High Sheriff, and tell him what's been going on here.'

'That's a long flight. Strikes me that it might be a good idea to have some company,' Jez said. 'And I promise not to holler in your ear.'

'You'd come with me, but what about the vents?'

'Hang the vents! I'm done scraping my knees to ribbons crawling about like a stupid dust rat,' she said. 'I'd just need to pick up some stuff from my treasure chest.'

It had crossed my mind how the sheriff would react to a kid showing up with a story about a squashed outlaw and a crooked sheriff, but if two of us showed up, and one of them was a mine worker who'd seen it all too; it might look better.

Jez was talking again, 'Besides, Ax is dead and the whole place is in a mess; I'd be amazed if I even have a job any more.'

I realised that could be my fault and apologised.

'Sorry? Heck, I'm not sorry. Took something like this to make me realise I need to get out of here while I still ain't crazy.' She thrust a stubby finger at me, grinning. 'And I ain't crazy.'

I smiled then turned to my horse. 'I'm OK with it, if Shy's OK to take another passenger.'

Moonshine whinnied. 'Fine, though I think we should get going. Be dark soon enough and it's a long flight to the top of the West Rock.'

We said nothing more and when we arrived at the side of the western arm, Moonshine took off carrying not one mount but two.

CHAPTER THIRTEEN

Fort Mordecai

Onwards and upwards we flew, to where the air warmed and tornadoes swirled in the distance; stopping near the edge of the western arm for a drink of cool creek water. We drank our fill then rested for a short while, watching the Mid-Rock Flyer steam inland towards a hazy Oretown that shimmered in the middle of the rock top. I thought about home and Yenene and part of me yearned to see her, just to make sure she was OK. But I couldn't think of it. I'd explain everything soon enough. Right now it was more important I see the High Sheriff as soon as possible.

We climbed higher and higher. At one point a couple of sky cowboys flew close by and one hollered, 'Where ya headed?'

'Mid-Rock Fort,' I called back.

'Mind how you go, young 'uns like

222

you shouldn't be flying so high up the rock, 'specially with the storms we been getting of late.'

'We hope to make it before nightfall,' Jez called.

'Then you'll need to get a move on.' He raised his cowboy hat as a disgruntled Moonshine, who seemed to have taken his comment as a slight to her flying ability, quickened her wing beats noticeably.

'Don't kill yourself on account of him, Shy. Cowboys always got something to say about nothing, Yenene says.'

We flew in silence for a while until Jez shouted in my ear. 'Y'know, I was wrong 'bout you.'

'You said you wouldn't do that.'

'Be wrong 'bout you?'

'Holler in my ear.'

She slapped my shoulder. 'Sorry, but I was still wrong about you.'

'What about?'

''Bout you being a bounty slay . . . seeker.'

'S'OK,' I replied. 'Guess if I was you, I probably wouldn't have believed me neither.'

Finally I caught sight of the top edge of the Mid-Rock, jutting out into the misty sky. We'd made it at last. The view was breathtaking. Up until then I'd only ever seen the Mid-Rock as it towered up past Oretown from the depths, like it had no base or summit. Rounding an outcrop, we saw a beautiful waterfall. Rainbow waters chased over the rock's edge to freefall into nothingness, the spray wetting our faces even this far away. It felt good after the long dusty climb. That last drink of creek water seemed like a lifetime ago.

The bad news, as we quickly discovered, was that the edge of the Mid-Rock was a vast gooey marshland and too treacherous to land on, which wasn't good as Moonshine badly needed to rest and drink.

'I'm OK, let's keep going,' she lied when I pointed this out.

We flew on beyond the marshland to where it was finally safe to land and from where we could see the outline of the city in the distance. Still Moonshine insisted we keep going.

Mid-Rock City was big and bustling with folk of all kinds. Shiny railway track was draped along one side of the city and ornamented with the biggest railway station I'd ever seen, complete with enormous clock tower. I wondered if it kept the right time—Oretown's clock had been wonky for years. Wagons and stagecoaches trundled noisily through the dusty streets that carved up the buildings into neat little squares; and wooden-planked walkways skirted a myriad of storefronts. Looking at the streets and buildings it was obvious stuff had been planned better here than back home in Oretown.

As we passed a brand-new, shiny black horse-drawn cart, Jez remarked, 'Wow, reckon I never seen such a swanky-looking cart.'

I was less impressed. 'I can just hear Pa when we used to pass a fancy cart, he'd say, "This ol' bone-shaker of a cart we're sittin' on will get us there just the same, and it's bought an' paid for." '

On the edge of town we made to go down a narrow street when an old man blocked our way.

'You're new to town right?' he remarked with a grin.

I hesitated but Jez was already nodding.

'You best keep moving. Ain't wise to go through the troll quarter before nightfall. Trolls don't take kindly to it.'

'Why?'

'They're sleeping.'

'Wow, they sure go to bed early,' said Jez.

'Go to bed?' the man grinned. 'They ain't been up yet. They sleep all day on account o' their eyes bein' sensitive to sunlight, then they make a racket during the night when ordinary decent folk are asleep.'

I had heard about trolls not liking daylight; Yenene said it was because their deeds were evil.

'Where ya headed?'

'The fort,' I told him.

'That's it on the rise of the hill. Best take the next street and turn left past Mid-Rock Bone Orchard.'

'We're obliged t'ya, sir,' I said and tipped my hat.

We followed the old man's directions and as we passed by the quite crowded graveyard we saw it—Fort Mordecai.

The fort was rectangular and made of solid, foot-thick timber; surrounded by a deep ditch with sharp, wooden spikes protruding from it, and high soil and boulder ramparts. At each corner there stood lofted lookout towers, enclosing a cavalryman wearing a neat

228

blue and yellow uniform and armed with a rifle.

We approached the sentry at the front gate and dismounted.

'We're here to see the High Sheriff,' I announced.

'Who are you?'

'Name's Will Gallows and this here's Jez.'

'Where you from?'

'Oretown.'

'What you want with him?

I was sure that this was just the guard being nosey rather than official questioning. 'Prefer to tell him that myself, if it's all right with you, on account of the information being sensitive.'

'The Hi . . .'

'And urgent,' I broke in.

He sighed. 'Stay here.'

He returned after a while and we were led inside, past the guard house and a cluster of one-storey, wooden buildings. I caught the smell of something nice cooking as we walked. There were groups of cavalrymen dotted throughout the fort: cleaning rifles, pistols, sabres; repairing what looked like a storm-damaged roof; lugging bags of grain and equipment, or just standing talking. One very hot and sweaty soldier sat shining the biggest pile of boots I'd ever seen. A skinny cavalryman who could only have been a year or two older than me, stood grooming a tall black mute-winged horse and said he'd keep an eye on Moonshine (not that she'd go anywhere but I thanked him).

The guard knocked on the door of a small cabin and disappeared, returning after a moment to usher us inside.

Jez and I stared at the tall figure standing, with his back toward us, at the window. He wore a knee-length, dark coat and when he turned I saw that he had a kind face, grey hair and moustache, and pale-blue eyes. The guard remained by the door, shouldering a long rifle.

The tall man extended a hand. 'Septimus Flynt, High Sheriff of the West Rock.'

I shook his hand, hearing all my knuckles crack.

'Thank you for seeing us, sir. My name is Will Gallows, my pa was Dan Gallows, Deputy Sheriff of Oretown. And this here's Jez, a worker from Deadrock Tin Mine.'

'Pleased to meet ya, sir.' Jez bowed a weird low bow, not coming up until I nudged her.

'We bring important news from Deadrock, sir,' I began. I'd prepared what I'd say on the long flight from Deadrock but it didn't take away the nerves now I was actually saying it. 'The Klondex gold mine in the deep mines has been re-opened by the outlaw, Noose Wormworx.'

The High Sheriff's eyebrows leaped up his forehead. 'Re-opened? How do you know?'

'We were there, sir, we saw it with our own eyes. Noose tried to kill us but we escaped. There was a shoot-out and Noose got killed.'

'Noose is dead?'

'During the gun battle I darted an ogre with a poison dart and it fell on him.'

'Stuff 'n' nonsense,' the guard broke

in. He addressed the High Sheriff, 'With respect, sir, everyone knows that mine is impenetrable. It would be impossible to re-open. Children and stories, I'd say.'

The High Sheriff raised a hand. 'That may be, but even children would be hard pushed to make up a story like this. And I knew the boy's father.'

I spotted the guard hurl me a scornful look then I went on: 'Thank you. After the shoot-out I ran into Sheriff Slugmarsh. At first he was OK with me, saying I'd done a great job, but then he changed—he got angry, real angry and I couldn't figure out why, till he told me.'

'Told you what?'

'That he's in on it with Noose, that Noose has been paying him to turn a blind eye to the deep-mine inspections.'

I was sure I detected a trace of disbelief on the High Sheriff's expression. 'Cleef Slugmarsh has been sheriff of Oretown for over thirty years,' he said. 'He's the most reputable sheriff we've ever . . .'

'Slugmarsh is a crook and a murderer,' I countered. 'He murdered my pa, confessed it to my face. He would've shot me too, but for Jez here.' I felt my cheeks flush with anger but fought it back. The sheriff didn't want to listen to bickering in his own office. I had to keep a cool head.

The guard stepped forward but the High Sheriff put up his hand. 'Go on.'

I took a deep breath and calmly told him about Jez's knife-throwing skills and an injured Slugmarsh, about Eldon and the quake-measuring device and about how Pa was caught up in it all.

After I'd finished there was a long silence. The High Sheriff ran a hand slowly from his forehead to his chin. When he spoke his voice brimmed with authority—and he called me by name.

'These are serious allegations, young Will. A sheriff dishonouring his badge is a breach of trust of the worst kind. Aside from what you've told us, the re-opening of that mine threatens the stability of the whole of the western arm. Thousands of lives could be at risk. This must be checked out

233

immediately. I want you both to stay at the fort. We'll contact your folks to let them know you're safe.' He paused, noticing our head shakes.

'Ain't got no folks,' Jez said first.

'I live with my grandmother, but I'd prefer to tell her about it afterwards, on account of her worrying.'

'That's OK. Get something to eat; the guard will show you where to go, and I think you could both use a visit to Doc Holliday too. I'll see you later.'

Not speaking, the guard led us through the fort to another cabin where we had hot beef pie and vegetables then, later on, we saw the doctor who put a salve on our hands and knees that stung like a clattersnake bite but afterwards felt good. We were at the stable visiting Moonshine when the High Sheriff appeared.

'How was the pie?'

'Good,' I replied.

'Better than good,' said Jez, licking her lips.

'We checked out Oretown's sheriff's office and there was no sign of Slugmarsh. A bystander informed us he'd been gone for some time. We'll ride down tomorrow morning after dawn, when the trolls have gone to bed. We don't want them poking their noses in as we ride out.'

'I understand.'

'In the meantime, I'll organise a group of men and sort out the equipment to reseal the mine. You both need to get some well-earned rest, not to mention that fine horse of yours. Were you shown your cabin?'

'Not yet.'

'Then c'mon, I'll take you there now.'

'I'd like to go with you tomorrow,' I said as we followed him out of the stable.

'Me too,' said Jez.

He frowned. 'You sure about that? It could get messy. Even with Noose gone, we can't assume the other trolls are just gonna let us through without some kind of resistance.'

'You heard what we been through, and we can show you where Slugmarsh is.'

'Well, I can't say it wouldn't be

handy having you along.' We stopped outside a small wooden cabin. 'Here we are. I'll see you in the morning, bright and early then.'

*　　　*　　　*

Inside, the cabin was pretty basic but clean and there were two comfortable beds under a small window.

'Getting dark,' I commented.

Jez flopped on her bed. 'Yeah, we just made it.'

'Whaddya think of the High Sheriff?'

'I like him.'

'You don't think he could be a crook too?'

'No. You?'

'Not the sheriff, the guard maybe but I dunno.'

'Yeah, who'd that guard think he was, stickin' his nose in where it didn't belong?'

'Maybe we should get some sleep,' I suggested. 'We got us a big day tomorrow.'

'I don't think I can,' Jez said. 'I ain't tired.'

236

I was. I lay down on my bed and shut my eyes till I heard Jez get up. 'Where you going?'

'For a walk.'

I sighed and turned over, but it wasn't long until my curiosity got the better of me and, with a sigh, I was on my feet following her out of the cabin.

Jez crossed the forecourt and climbed the ladder to the lookout tower. I climbed after her. The bearded lookout guard greeted us then glanced anxiously down into the courtyard.

'Ya ain't s'posed to be up here,' he said in a low voice. 'High Sheriff sees ya, I'll be in trouble.'

'Oh, just for a while, please,' Jez pleaded.

'You're the kids come to see the High Sheriff?'

'Yeah.' I gazed out over Mid-Rock City. The view was spectacular. My eye was drawn to a crowded noisy street on the outskirts of the city. 'What's all the commotion over that part of town?'

He smiled. 'Troll quarter openin' up for business: drinkin', brawlin' and dancin' till sun up. Maybe even another riot like last week.'

'Riot?'

'Better believe it. Becomin' all too frequent of late.'

'City's changin' for the worst, trolls are overrunnin' the place. Speakin of which, you're for Deadrock in the morning, ain't ya?'

'Yes, we're going back to seal the deep mines.'

'That's quite a journey; you should get yourselves some shut-eye.'

I figured we'd overstayed our welcome and nudged Jez. 'We'll be on our way, goodnight.'

'Goodnight, and keep your wits about you tomorrow in that hell hole.'

CHAPTER FOURTEEN

Troll Fury

The next morning I woke early, glad to see it was daylight. I hadn't slept well. The noises of the night—the tinkle of a distant piano, troll voices squabbling and gunfire—were now replaced by the sound of horses' hooves and cart wheels being drawn over gravel, and cavalrymen's voices.

Jez's bed was empty, though I wasn't surprised. It was like she didn't need sleep. I got up. My legs ached from too much vent crawling and I hobbled like an old man over to the door.

Outside, even though it was early, it looked like all the soldiers were up and busying themselves with the daily activities of the fort. Some lugged spades and picks and thick rope that I guessed must be to reseal the deep mines. I recognised a few of them from yesterday and we exchanged greetings.

I found Jez in the mess cabin along

with some other soldiers, tucking into a plate full of eggs over beans and drinking coffee.

'You're up then.' She smiled, taking another mouthful of beans.

A kindly-faced lady brought me my breakfast and a mug of coffee.

'I couldn't sleep much either,' Jez went on, as though sensing my grogginess. 'S'lot quieter on the side of the ridge. That is if there ain't no storms. High Sheriff asked if we were still OK 'bout comin'.'

'What did you say?'

'Course we are, just try an' stop us.'

I smiled. 'When do we ride out?'

'This mornin' soon as we eat.'

After breakfast Jez went back to the cabin and I went to find Shy. She was already saddled and standing alongside twenty or so other horses that stood loaded with equipment. Soldiers busied themselves checking tack and sharpening sabres.

Shy didn't like to critter chatter in front of the horses but nudging me away from them, she said softly, 'I wish my pa could see me now. Do you know that loads of the other horses thought I was a new trainee sky-cavalry horse, can you believe it?'

'Reckon I could, Shy. You got the makings of a fine sky-cavalry horse: spirit, strength, and you flew up to Mid-Rock City without a grumble.'

She whinnied and I knew that meant someone was coming. I turned round. It was the High Sheriff.

'This is just some of the lighter stuff,' the High Sheriff said, striding up behind me. 'The heavier stuff's already on its way on the early train to Deadrock. It'll be there to meet us at the freight station. Did you have a good sleep?'

'Yeah, breakfast was good too. Thank you.'

'I doubt you'll want to, but you're welcome to rest that fine horse of yours and fly one of the cavalry horses down.'

'Thanks but Shy doesn't like to miss out on anything.'

'And your friend?'

I thought about Jez's hollering in my ear. Sure be quieter if she rode with the soldiers. But I knew she'd want to come with us. 'S'OK, be easier on the way down so Shy should be OK carrying the two of us again.'

The High Sheriff didn't seem to be in any mood for hanging around and soon we were riding out the fort gates, dust trailing into the air behind us.

I felt a rush of pride riding through Mid-Rock City with the sky cavalry, clad in their neat uniforms, sandwiched between two flag bearers holding bright yellow flags.

Near the edge of the rock the High Sheriff gave the order to prepare for flight and, keeping in formation with the others, I cracked the reins, spurring Moonshine into a gallop.

The flight down seemed a lot quicker. If not a cavalryman, I was fast becoming a pro sky cowboy, recognising some of the crags and ridges in the rock face from yesterday. A few storms swirled in the distance but they were much too far away to present any real danger. We didn't stop at the western arm but kept flying. Shy didn't bat an eyelid. I knew that even if she was thirsty she'd no intention of letting the other horses know.

At the Deadrock tunnel the High Sheriff raised an arm, crying, 'I gave orders to the Railroad Company to halt the Flyer in Deadrock station until we were all safely through.' And landing, he plunged into the gaping hole, the rest of us streaming single file after him.

Passing the catacombs, I was sure I could hear Henk's manic laughter echo faintly among the tombs, and I felt sad, realising I'd never see him again. Earlier I'd informed the High Sheriff about the large quantity of stykes in the tunnel but he assured me that the two scouts who always rode up front would be on the lookout for the tapered terrors.

The tin mine, when we drew near, was peculiarly quiet. The skull-topped, iron gates lay open and there was no sign of a burly troll guard at the entrance. Some of the men broke off at the freight station to fetch the equipment. I rode with the others to the entrance where I dismounted. From here we would proceed on foot, leading into the mine only those horses that were required to carry equipment. I left Shy at the entrance and Jez and I followed in a group behind the High Sheriff. I didn't like the look on his face. I was pretty sure he was thinking what I was thinking—where was everybody? So far the only folk we'd seen were a group of jeering trolls on the outskirts of Deadrock as we'd passed nearby, obviously unhappy at our intrusion.

We marched on; the clip-clop of hooves, the rattle of cart wheels and the stomp of soldiers' boots, the only noises in the semi-darkness.

Eventually we reached the end of the main tunnel, trudging into a well-lit cavern with three further tunnels branching off it—one of which was the tunnel I'd taken the previous day when I'd come across the mine wraith. I spoke to inform the High Sheriff that the widest of the three would take us to the deep mines.

And then they struck.

There was a loud roar from the back of our posse. Heart thumping, I bolted round; an outcrop of rock on the mine wall provided me with foothold to see over the other soldiers. The roar was not that of a mine wraith but of a host of frantic, angry trolls: the guttural rasp of rattlethroats and the hiss of snake-bellies, as the lifeless mine air was suddenly quickened with noise and chaos.

A single, deafening gunshot spurred the High Sheriff to bellow, 'Holster your guns, it's too dangerous, the ricochets will kill us all—use your sabres. Use your sabres!'

There was a high-pitched squeal of steel as sabres were drawn from scabbards then the clang of metal; pickaxe on sabre, followed by screams and snarling and the crashing of weapons.

Ambush. It had been too quiet for a reason. The High Sheriff, his sword already drawn, darted back through the other men to the thick of the battle. He'd been expecting it, I thought.

But there was no time to think as out of the widest of the three tunnels another army of troll miners poured from the gloom, brandishing pickaxes and sledge hammers and rock hammers and spades. One of them broke off from the rest, charging towards me. Horror-struck, I ducked as the pick he wielded embedded itself in the rock just above my head, sending splinters of rock and dust over my neck and shoulders. The troll cursed, pulling the axe free. Again he struck, only with more ferocity and in a downwards motion, hoping to slice into my head, but I only just managed to dodge to one side, stumbling as I did to tumble on the floor. I glanced up to see the troll, with a loud hiss, raise the tool above his head, grinning as he anticipated the delight of finishing me off. Desperately I drove both soles of my boots hard into the troll's knee, hearing it crack on impact. He screamed in agony, teetering backwards in a painful dance and I was on my feet, grabbing a saddlewood branch from its wall holder to thrust in his face, disorientating him just long enough for me to steal his weapon.

'Ya got him good,' I heard Jez yell from her own mini battle with a gangly troll. She held out a sword and was swaying from side to side in front of him. He clutched a spade and mirrored her movements, but he soon tired of her trickery and lashed out, but she was too quick for him and easily parried the blow.

A hammer-wielding troll spun towards me out of the darkness and I braced myself, readying my weapon, but to my relief I saw his belly was sodden with blood and he crumpled at my feet.

Panting, I looked around. The mine was littered with cut-down trolls. Were we winning? At this end, anyway—I couldn't see how the High Sheriff was getting on further back in the tunnel.

'Will, behind you!' Jez cried.

I spun round, instinctively angling and raising my axe as a troll pickaxe crashed into it. Snarling, the troll struck again with ferocious power. I felt the strength drain from my arms as he rained blow after blow. Jez tried to help; thrusting her sword at him but the troll was relentless. I backed up until I hit the mine wall and could go no further. Grinning, he closed in. But as he did so, two or three sword tips appeared from the semi-darkness, blocking him, then four . . . five, glinting purple in the saddlewood light and I was aware that it was suddenly quieter. The troll cursed and dropped his weapon as soldiers clustered round him. The battle was over.

'You all right?' Jez appeared through the group of soldiers, wide-eyed and face glistening with sweat, still clutching her sword.

'I'm OK, you?'

'Yeah.'

The High Sheriff strode into the light, gasping for breath, his face bloodied and dirty.

'Thank the spirits you kids are all right. Sorry I left you, didn't count on it being a double-sided attack.'

'S'OK, we held the varmits,' said Jez. 'Place looks like a troll-bone orchard.'

'We could do with the likes of you both in the sky cavalry.'

I couldn't believe my ears; the High Sheriff himself reckoned we'd make good soldiers in the sky cavalry. I glanced at Jez, her face was beaming through the grubbiness. I just wished Pa was still alive—I knew he'd have been proud to hear stuff like this.

The High Sheriff informed us that we had lost three men and a few injured were being taken back to the entrance. Twenty trolls had been slaughtered.

'This was a waste of life,' he added. 'These trolls fought half-heartedly, a dispirited bunch.'

I couldn't believe my ears. I thought my troll had fought very whole-heartedly.

'It's obvious a lot has happened here, there's an air of confusion and fear.' He sheathed his sabre. 'We'll advance to the deep mines, to finish this matter, then we'll hold counsel with the mayor of Deadrock.'

Journeying on through the labyrinth of tunnels, we soon arrived at the deep mines and I found myself stepping anxiously into the big cavern for the second time in as many days. My gaze fell immediately on the stone mill wheel that had almost squashed my bones, then behind it to where the ogre lay, not breathing.

The High Sheriff didn't waste any time giving the men orders for sealing the mine. Carts were unloaded and ropes tied to wooden posts and ceiling supports that when dragged away by the strong horses would collapse the roof, blocking the mine for good.

I was walking close to the outside of the cavern when, suddenly, I felt a rope drape round my shoulders. My first thought was that it was one of the cavalrymen fooling around but I quickly realised something wasn't quite right when the twine was yanked painfully tight around the tops of my arms, digging into my flesh. Smelling the faint whiff of Boggart's Breath whiskey, I turned to see the face of my captor appear from an alcove, gold tooth flashing in the saddlewood light—Slugmarsh!

Heart pounding, I felt an icy chill shoot up my spine. The last time I'd seen him, he'd been lying on the cavern floor near the vent hole with Jez's bone-handled knife protruding from his back. Seemed he'd made a pretty good recovery—and judging by the scowl on his face, the episode had made him a whole lot nastier.

He held a gun to my head.

At his feet I noticed a saddlebag stuffed with gold.

'Well, if it ain't the high 'n' mighty Sheriff, Septimus Flynt, come to sort everything out,' he drawled, roping me in like a wayward calf.

There was a sudden rasp of metal as a few soldiers drew their sabres but the High Sheriff signalled for them to hold their strike.

'Someone needed to, Slugmarsh. You sure ain't been doin' your job. You were meant to make sure the deep mines were kept sealed, not help a snake-belly to re-open them.'

'See you managed to survive my little ambush—should've known those dumb trolls couldn't do anything right.'

The High Sheriff took a few cautious steps towards us. 'Why, Slugmarsh? Why'd you dishonour your badge?'

'Back off, Flynt, or wear the kid's brains.'

'It's over; you've had your fun, now give it up. You're badly wounded, you need a doctor.'

'The hell it's over. And what I need is for you to get outta my face,' he spat. 'This mine ain't none o' yours any more. What goes on in troll quarters oughta stay in troll quarters.'

'Not when it affects the whole rock,' the High Sheriff countered.

'All that stuff about minin' weakenin' the rock is a pile of dung. Deadrock's built inside a cavern in the middle of the mid-rock yet I don't see the mid-rock startin' to cave in.' His voice changed, toned with a hint of desperation. 'We could run this gold mine together, Flynt. Think about it, we'd be rich—filthy rich!'

'Don't play the idiot, Slugmarsh. You know as well as I do that the deep mines run into one of the thinnest parts of the West Rock, where the western arm joins the mid-rock. If this mine ain't closed the consequences could be disastrous.'

'You're a fool, Flynt, a danged fool.'

'See you're planning on leaving with a few nuggets in your saddle.' The High Sheriff pointed to the bag at Slugmarsh's feet.

'Looks like I ain't got much choice. Now if you'll excuse us, me an' the boy here's goin' for a little ride.' He lifted the saddle bag and tossed it over the nearest horse. 'Get on the horse, kid.'

'You can't run for ever, Slugmarsh,' the High Sheriff warned. 'We'll catch up with you, you can count on it.'

I swung into the saddle of the cavalry horse. Then Slugmarsh got on behind me and pushed my face into the horse's mane. 'You boys enjoy yourselves. Just be careful the whole dang lot don't come in on top of you. Oh, and don't think of following—if I hear a horse pursuin' us then the boy dies.'

Next thing, gloomy cave walls and saddlewood lamps blurred past as we rode out of the deep mines, passing the dead bodies of the troll miners.

Slugmarsh kept his hand forcefully on my neck, shoving my head against the horse's mane so hard that I found it hard to breathe and the rope, which was too tight, dug into my arms. I felt dizzy and sick as we rode quickly through the deep mine tunnels, the tin mine seams and finally out the mine entrance, then onward out of Deadrock tunnel.

*   *   *

We had just galloped out of the tunnel and flown into open sky when a crazy thing happened. Slugmarsh thrust my head forward again and I felt a sudden rush of anger. The rope that bound me was secured round my upper arms, so I could move my lower arms from the elbow down and I'd brought my right hand over to try and relieve the pressure where it dug into my left arm, when I became aware of a strong tingling sensation. I'd never felt it before and it quickly became more intense—like a burning but from my hands, not the rope.

255

The natural thing would've been to let go of the rope but I didn't, I clung tighter . . . tighter, until I felt the twisted fibres start to blacken and break up below my fingers. Heart hammering in my chest, my mind raced with it. What was this? Had I some kind of magic after all that I wasn't aware of? The elf lamplighter from the Flyer, who had conjured fire from his hands, sprang into my head. Moments later, and with a puff of

smoke, the rope broke and I was miraculously free. I had, however, only moments to get my head round my new-found power as with a loud whistle the Flyer suddenly appeared,  thundering round a steep bend behind us. The cavalry horse neighed loudly,

pulling its head away and beating its wings faster, all of which incensed Slugmarsh, who lashed it hard with the whip. I felt sorry for the horse. A fierce whiplash could break the skin, at best leaving tender striped bruises for days.

'OK, kid, this is where you get off,' he rasped. And he pushed me, expecting me to fall like a bound helpless calf. But I shot out both my newly freed arms, grabbing blindly for the saddle, for anything. Unfortunately, what I grabbed slid off the horse with me—it was the saddle bag full of gold. I heard Slugmarsh curse as he watched his fortune slip away.

I dropped like a diving eagle through the air.

Numb with fear and vision blurring, I waited to hit either a rocky outcrop or the ground below. Miraculously I hit neither. Instead I landed with a thud onto the roof of the Flyer, the gold still in my grasp.

Slugmarsh closed in. The horse, browbeaten by the whipping, gave in; flying low over the carriage I lay sprawled on. I watched the Sheriff dismount in midair, keeping one foot in the stirrup. When he was low enough, he leaped onto the carriage. I was mystified as to how he didn't crash straight through the roof but maybe that was too much to hope for. Clutching his six-shot blaster he got to his feet, struggling to find his balance amid the bumpy track and strong wind. His shirt was stained red by the knife wound, his face too, where he'd run a bloodied hand over his forehead. My back ached from the fall. Yet somehow I got to my feet—but only to stare into the barrel of Slugmarsh's gun.

'Give me the gold!'

'So you can put a bullet in me? Don't think so.'

'I got no time for heroics, kid. Give me that saddle bag.'

I dangled it over the edge of the train. 'Shoot me and we both tumble into the Wastelands.'

'I should've put a bullet in you when I had the chance, or maybe even when you walked into my office,' Slugmarsh yelled, his gold tooth glinting in the sunlight.

'Maybe your judgement isn't what it was,' I sneered.

'Give me the gold—NOW!'

Slugmarsh, his face reddening, straightened his arm and started squeezing the trigger.

'Naaaeeeeeeeee!' Moonshine let out the shrillest of whinnies, plummeting out of nowhere towards Slugmarsh, her front hooves outstretched. He bolted around, ducking his head but lost his balance. He fell sideways, dropping the gun, his bulk sending him rolling over the low rail—over the outside edge of the carriage top. He grasped the rail to dangle above the gaping void below.

I crawled towards him, extending a hand. But he spat on it. 'If you were a real bounty slayer, you'd finish me off. But you can't even do that right, can you?' he taunted.

I withdrew my hand. 'If you were a real sheriff I wouldn't have to.'

The Flyer gave a shrill whistle as it thundered round a bend in the rock.

'Very honourable, boy, spoken like a future sheriff of Oretown—'cept Oretown ain't got a future.' He laughed scornfully then coughed. 'Oretown's finished. Klondex and Noose have hacked the heart from the western stem. Noose especially has botched the re-opening. It's only a matter o' time . . .'

A gust of wind blew and the bar creaked, bowing under the sheriff's weight.

'Me, though, I ain't finished. No, sir, this ain't the end y'know. I plan on coming back for you . . .'

With a sudden clunk, one side of the bar the sheriff clung to tore from its housing and bent outwards and downwards taking him with it, his hands sliding slowly towards the far end.

'Better believe it,' he ranted on. 'I'm coming back as the biggest, ugliest wraith you ever seen to haunt you . . .' The rail was running out and he clung one-handed now, swaying in the wind. 'Haunt you in the middle of the night.' Slowly, his hand slid from the rail. 'Sweet dreams, boy!' He plummeted into the void, 'Sweet . . . dreeeeeeeams!'

I sat, clutching my knees, staring out over the carriage tops, watching Moonshine descend up ahead to make a perfect landing on the carriage, and behind her another cavalry horse—the High Sheriff's.

The High Sheriff dismounted and made his way towards me, calling, 'Is he gone?'

'Over the side,' I shouted back.

'No more than he deserved. You OK?'

'Yeah.'

He eyed the tan-leather bag near my feet. 'Gold didn't drop with him, I see.'

'S'all here, sir.'

'We'll bring it back to the fort and put it to good use. Maybe even use it to fortify the western arm from the mining damage.'

'What about the mine?' I asked.

'Almost done, place is probably cavin' in on itself as we speak. It's over, Will. We can all go home.'

Moonshine, her wings outstretched, trotted carefully towards me over the carriage top. 'I kinda like the sound of that.'

Getting to my feet, I gave her a rub between the ears. 'I do too.'

CHAPTER FIFTEEN

Calm after the Storm

Phoenix Creek burned under a noontime sun with all the ranch hands sheltered in shady parts, eating bread and dried-beef strips.

We sat in the kitchen: myself, Yenene, Jez and the High Sheriff—who had accompanied me back home with a few soldiers. Yenene was avoiding my gaze; she'd hardly spoken a word to me since we'd got back. It didn't help that the High Sheriff was in no hurry to return to Fort Mordecai but now sat with his boots off, devouring a bowl of hot stew.

'Mighty tasty stew, ma'am,' he said, hungrily spooning another mouthful past his moustache.

'Sure gonna take a while for this to sink in,' Yenene repeated for, I'd lost count how many times. 'Told me he was goin' fishin'. Pha! And after me wastin' my time, baking a pie for his

264

uncle in Gung Village.'

'Don't be too hard on the boy; as well as getting rid of one of the biggest bandits on the rock, he might just have saved the western arm from breaking off like a rotten branch of saddlewood.'

Had I? I wondered. *Oretown's finished!* Slugmarsh's words echoed through my head: There was no doubt the rock tremors were getting more frequent and, even if the High Sheriff could somehow strengthen it, I wondered how much time the western arm had left before it did break off into the wastelands . . . years . . . seasons . . . days?

'Course, there'll be a reward,' the High Sheriff went on.

Yenene frowned, lifting a pot from the stove. 'Reward?'

'The boy didn't kill Noose but he was responsible for bringing about his downfall, so the bounty on Noose's head belongs to him.'

I figured that might bring her round—the barn roof was just about ready to collapse it was so badly in need of repair—but she just refilled his empty dish, muttering, 'Can't think about that right now.'

Finishing my stew, I got up. 'I'll start on my chores, Grandma.' I was glad of the excuse to get out of the stuffy atmosphere. 'Jez, you wanna come and see the ranch?'

'Sure.' She took both our bowls over to the sink. 'Thanks for the lunch, ma'am.'

As I passed him, the High Sheriff offered me his hand with a smile and I shook it. 'Goodbye, sir.'

'Goodbye, Will, and thank you. You're welcome to come visit us anytime; you know I've offered Jez a job in the fort kitchen.'

I didn't and the news lifted the gloomy feeling I'd had since getting home. Jez was a good friend and I'd been worried she'd go back to the Wastelands or somewhere where I'd never see her again.

The High Sheriff went on. 'You might even think about joining us too some day, sky cavalry's always look—' But he broke off when Yenene glared at him.

Jez and I went outside and headed past the stable.

'How's Shy?' she asked.

'She's fine. Tired, but fine.' We looked in on her and found her curled up asleep on some hay.

'So you'll be working at the fort?'

'For a while, yeah, though I'm not sure about cooking. Hope to get me a job working with the horses. I've enjoyed spending time with Shy. What about you? What are you going to do?'

'Learn 'bout elf magic,' I answered. 'I'm not stupid enough to ask my grandma now, she's madder than a skinned clattersnake. But when things blow over I'm gonna go and see my Uncle Crazy Wolf in Gung-Choux Village and talk to him. It could get me out of a pickle if I'm caught up in something in the future . . .'

267

'You planning on going on another bounty hunt? Cos if you are I'd go with you.'

I shook my head. 'But if I was, I'd let you know. We were a pretty good team.'

'Sounds like you're gonna be busy, anyway.'

I sighed, 'With branding the herd, yeah.'

She put a hand to the scorpion pendant round her neck and smiled. 'Thanks for this.'

'You're welcome.'

We walked round the ranch buildings for a while: I introduced Jez to some of the ranch hands, until I heard some commotion over at the farm house and realised it was the High Sheriff and the other soldiers preparing the horses, getting ready to leave. Yenene was nowhere to be seen.

'I best go with them,' Jez said.

I nodded and we started back.

*　　　*　　　*

I watched them all ascend into the sky.

Jez waved furiously from the back of the High Sheriff's mount. When they were nothing more than tiny dots in the sky, I turned to head back towards the ranch when I almost bumped into Yenene.

I could tell by her stone expression that she was still mad. 'They've gone,' I said stupidly, as she'd most likely watched them fly off. 'I'll get to my chores.'

As I passed her, she grumbled, 'Where'd I go wrong, Will?'

I paused, frowning. 'What do you mean?'

'I raise you up to be a sky cowboy an' the first chance you get you're pullin' wanted posters off the sheriff's office and goin' bounty huntin'.'

'I did it for Pa,' I said solemnly. 'I figured you'd understand.'

'Oh, I understand all right. I understand that it's a lawman's job to go catchin' outlaws.'

'I know, but what if the lawman's crooked too?'

'Then there's the mayor, the sky cavalry, the High Sheriff . . .'

'It'd been a whole year and nothing had been done to catch Pa's killer, I . . .'

'S'only by the grace of the Great Spirit you're not buried in Oretown bone orchard beside him, young man.'

'I know you're angry with me but I had to do it.'

'Heck, it wasn't just what you did, Will, it was the way you did it. All the sneakin' around, the lie tellin'.'

'I'm sorry about the lies but if I'd told you the truth, would you have let me go?'

'No.'

'See.'

She sighed. 'Look, I am glad you're home. I'm angry yes and tomorrow I'll be angry and the day after that, but I'm still glad you're home.'

'I'm glad to *be* home,' I said. 'And I promise I won't even go near the sheriff's office, and I'll get caught up with my chores.'

She nodded, the faintest of smiles cracking on her wrinkled face. 'I don't doubt that, you're a work horse like your pa, that's for sure. Which reminds me, that fence you mended is holding up real well, 'cept the two fences either side of it are broken now.'

'I'll take Shy over to take a look later, when she wakes up.'

'That'll do. I'll see you at supper.' And she walked back in the direction of the ranch house. 'Oh, be sure an' keep an eye out for wolves. There's a pack o' them still hanging around over there.'

'I will.'

I was heading for the outbuildings to find the other ranch hands when a faint whistle made me turn round. A distant plume of white steam streaked the sky, the Flyer thundering towards the rock's edge to begin its descent to Deadrock. I watched it for a moment, glad that I didn't have to spend another night in that cold, gloomy underground world, fumbling my way around in the dim saddlewood light and breathing the stale air. I was glad, too, that I'd never have to squeeze through another hole in the side of the rock again, to crawl along twisting, rat-infested mine vents that seemed to go for ever.

I was home, and tonight the only thing I'd be crawling into was my warm, comfortable bed.

*With grateful acknowledgement to:
Carolyn Whitaker of London
Independent Books, Charlie Sheppard
and Eloise King of Andersen Press*